THE
SECRET OATH

4

THE RUGENDO RHINOS SERIES

THE
SECRET OATH

SHEL ARENSEN

Kregel
Publications

The Secret Oath

© 2003 by Shel Arensen

Published by Kregel Publications, a division of Kregel, Inc., P.O. Box 2607, Grand Rapids, MI 49501.

Cover illustration: David Du

ISBN 0-8254-2040-7

Printed in the United States of America

03 04 05 06 07 / 5 4 3 2 1

To my son, Heath,
whose love for Africa as a child inspired me
to write this book to capture those memories
of an African childhood enjoyed.

CHAPTER ONE

THE TREE HOUSE

We entered the thick forest following a path that snaked its way between the giant trees. It was actually an animal trail made by dik-diks, small rabbit-size antelopes that raided our cabbage patch. We stalked quietly. I used the barrel of my air rifle to push aside overhanging ferns.

"I see one," hissed Matt, our leader.

We were the Rugendo Rhinos, a club of five boys who lived at a mission station called Rugendo in the Kenya highlands.

The dik-dik ducked into the undergrowth and disappeared. Jon Freedman turned and frowned at Matt.

"You scared him before I could shoot," he chided. Jon loved hiking, hunting, and trapping, but he became impatient with the rest of us when we stumbled into wait-a-bit thorns and started yelling and scaring off our prey and other things like that. His parents, both doctors, had come to Rugendo the year before. At first they worried that Jon would miss TV when they took him away from America. Now they worry whether Jon will ever leave Africa.

"Shoot faster, " Matt retorted. Matt Chadwick liked to be first

7

at everything except schoolwork. He moved as fast as a Thomson's gazelle's tail. He always had to be doing something like chasing a honey guide bird through the forest to see if it would lead us to a beehive. Because of his never-ending energy, we accepted him as our leader.

Jon shrugged and continued to stalk dik-diks. We Rhinos followed.

The year before, Matt had announced we should form a club after watching the Rhino Charge, a four-wheel-drive care race across some of the toughest bush in Kenya. "We can call ourselves the Rugendo Rhinos because we crash through the bush on our bikes like those Land Rovers and Land Cruisers at the Rhino Charge."

After twenty more minutes of trying to creep up on the wily little dik-diks with their spiky two-inch horns, Matt called for us to halt. "This is useless. We'll never shoot a dik-dik. Let's go to our tree fort." The tree fort had been Matt's idea too.

"I agree," I said. "Let's go to the fort." I'm more of a follower. I love doing things as much as Matt, but I'm not very good at making decisions. I prefer following Matt's suggestions. My name is Dean Sandler, and the day Matt suggested we build a tree fort, I had backed him all the way. He said we should build it in the big wild fig tree in the ravine.

"I still wish we could have built a bigger tree house," Matt said as we arrived at the base of the tree.

"Hold on a minute," Dave Krenden said in his slow, methodical way. He was the fourth member of our group and adjusted his black-rimmed glasses as he spoke. "I designed a solid two-room tree house that wouldn't collapse, remember?" Dave, tall, thin, and serious, took after his dad, who worked as a builder at the mission hospital.

Kamau looked from Matt to Dave as they argued. His dad worked with Mr. Krenden as a carpenter. Kamau had joined our Rhino club during our adventure in capturing some daring carjackers.

Jon climbed the tree and threw down the rope ladder. We clambered into our tree fort, which served as our secret clubhouse.

It had taken a week of hard work to build the tree house the year before. Dave's dad insisted on inspecting it before he would let us use it, and I could see he was really proud of Dave. After being sure the tree house was safe, he said in a low voice, "I have no idea where I am. Could you boys please direct me to the Rugendo mission station?" Then he winked at us. We all grinned. We knew our secret would be safe with him.

Matt looked around as we sat down in the tree fort. "Since we're here, we might as well have a club meeting," Matt said. "Are we all here, Dean?"

"Yes," I answered. Doing roll call was one of my jobs as secretary. I had been elected club secretary because I got good grades in English. I didn't tell anyone about the bad grades I got in handwriting. I figured if I could read what I'd written, it didn't really matter. Unfortunately, there were many times when even I couldn't read my notes.

"We have one thing to discuss," Matt said, starting the meeting. "You know how Jill and her Cheetah club almost beat us in the case of the carjackers. We need to come up with some ways to be sure they don't get ahead of the Rhinos."

"I don't want the girls to beat us," Dave commented, "but without a real mystery to solve, it's hard to plan ways to beat them."

Dave's logic stumped Matt, who grumbled, "Well, if anything comes up, I want us Rhinos to be ready. We can't have Jill and her Cheetahs saying they're better than us."

Suddenly Jon tilted his head toward the window. He stood up and peered outside. "A flock of pigeons!" he pointed out. We closed our meeting hastily and climbed down from the tree house.

We slipped into the forest, following the pigeons. I carried my air rifle in my right hand with a pocket full of pellets. Jon carried his pellets under his tongue. "Easier to get out quickly," he told us one day. What he said was true. In the heat of a hunt, I always had difficulty separating my pellets from the candy wrappers, dried gum, black pieces of volcanic glass, and various other treasures that filled my pockets. But I worried that pellets in the mouth could give me lead poisoning, so I still kept my ammo in my pocket.

Kamau walked at my side, carrying a slingshot made out of a Y-shaped branch covered with tiny strips of black inner tube rubber. Two larger rubber straps met in the middle at a soft strip of leather. Kamau would slip a smooth pebble into the leather and pinch it between his right thumb and index finger as he pulled it back and aimed at his target. He also carried a throwing club in his belt with a baseball-sized knob at the end of the two-foot handle. Kamau could kill a bird, a rabbit, or even a puff adder with that club.

Jon led the way. We came to a grassy glade in the middle of the forest, and Jon spotted the tree where the pigeons had landed. We called them pigeons. My dad, a bird watcher, had told me the correct name was ring-necked dove. I brought this up at one of our club meetings. Everyone agreed we should call our quarry by its proper name, but when we hunted, we always slipped back and called them pigeons.

"There's one," Jon whispered. "It landed in that wild olive tree over there." The tree had scaly bark and pale green-gray leaves.

"I can't see it," I whispered to Matt.

He smiled. "Why do you think I let Jon lead our hunts?"

We inched to within twenty yards of the tree. Then I saw it—the plumpest ring-necked dove I'd ever seen. I pointed and whispered, "I see it!" At that moment it flew into the air, wings flapping loudly. Jon gave me a nasty look. I felt terrible, but before I could even apologize, Jon had swung his head to follow the flight of the bird.

"OK, it's landed again," he said. "Now, this time let's be quiet and avoid any sudden movements."

"My lips are sealed," I said, making a zipping motion across my mouth. "I'm sorry about scaring the pigeon."

Jon scowled and began stalking the bird again. Matt followed him, but Dave patted me on the shoulder. "It's OK," he whispered. "I hadn't even seen the pigeon yet when you spoke up and scared it."

"I hadn't seen it either," Kamau admitted.

I smiled my appreciation to them, but I kept extra quiet. Jon silently led our stalk on the fat pigeon or dove or whatever that gray bird was called. Jon wanted to call it 'supper.' When we got close enough, Jon leaned his gun in the crotch of a branch in a low bush and aimed. But before he could squeeze the trigger, the bird again flew up in a flurry of flapping wings.

This time it hadn't been me who spooked the bird. It was a Kikuyu man dressed in traditional animal skin clothing. He shuffled down the path to our left. He had gray hair and carried a goatskin bag in one hand and a squirming kid goat under his other arm. We watched as he hurried past without noticing us. Then he was gone.

"I wonder who that was?" Matt asked.

"He looked like a witch doctor," I answered.

Matt laughed at me. "Just because he's wearing skin clothing doesn't mean he's a witch doctor."

"Well, not many people wear traditional clothing anymore," I answered. "But my dad says witch doctors often put on their old clothes for ceremonies."

Kamau's eyes widened as we argued.

"What do you think, Kamau?" I asked. "Was that man what you Kikuyu call a *mundu mugo*? A witch doctor?"

Kamau gulped. "Maybe," he answered. Beads of sweat formed on Kamau's forehead, and his eyes roved back and forth. I remembered how Kamau and Jon had both been cursed by a witch doctor and had almost died from a mysterious disease.

"Can we get on with the hunt?" Jon reminded us. "I want to eat that pigeon tonight. See that tree? The pigeon landed near the top." We stalked the bird, easing our way through the bushes, but the pigeon flapped away before we got near enough to aim.

"Let's take a break," Matt suggested. We sat down under a tree, unbuckled our canteens, and drank. Kamau looked around nervously. He had stuffed his sling shot into his belt and now carried his club.

"Are you okay, Kamau?" I asked.

He nodded, but I could tell he was lying.

As we rested, Dave heard the sound first. "What's that noise?" he asked.

"The noise is you talking," Matt answered, laughing at his own wit.

"No, I'm serious," said Dave. "Listen."

We listened closely. I heard it. "It sounds like a drum," I said. "BOM-tum-tum-BOM-tum-tum-BOM, like that."

The others heard it too.

"I wonder what it is?" Dave asked again.

"Let's find out," Matt said.

"What about the pigeons?" Jon asked.

"We'll go after them later," Matt answered.

"I'm not sure this is a good idea," Kamau put in.

Matt ignored Kamau and led the way. We would walk for a while and then stop and listen to be sure we were heading in the right direction. Kamau hung back, reluctant to follow. Maybe we should have followed his example.

We soon found the path the old man had been on. It was easier to walk on the path than to keep bush barging. Besides, the sound seemed to be coming from straight up the path.

Ahead of us, the path opened into a clearing where a small group of people had gathered. Someone was beating a drum. A fire flickered, and the old man who had scared our pigeon was butchering the goat.

Matt signaled for all of us to get down. We wormed our way off the path to the edge of the clearing. The old man gutted the dead goat and gave parts of the stomach and intestines to the wide-eyed, sweating people in front of him. They ate the pieces of meat raw and said something in Kikuyu.

My back felt like a gray hairy caterpillar was crawling down it. I was sure we had stumbled onto a secret Kikuyu oathing ceremony. The old man we'd seen really was a *mundu mugo*. My dad had told me about the custom of oathing, which bound the Kikuyu people in making promises or covenants in their traditional culture. It had been the binding force during the Mau Mau fight for independence. The Kikuyu freedom fighters administered the blood oath, which forced people to promise to support the fight against colonialism. They also had to promise not to betray the freedom fighters who hid in the forests to battle against the British army.

That had been years before. Kenya had won its independence now, but my dad said the oathing was being revived for political reasons.

I looked at Kamau. "It's an oathing ceremony, isn't it?" I whispered.

He nodded, eyes rolling wildly. "We should leave now!"

I crawled next to Matt. "It's an oathing ceremony," I hissed in his ear. "Let's get out of here or we'll be in trouble. It's a tribal secret." In my nervousness, I'm afraid I hissed the *S* in *secret*.

The old man whirled his head and stared right at the bush where we were hiding. He shouted something, and two young men walked toward us.

Matt stood up and yelled, "Run!"

SAFARI RALLY

We ran like rabbits trying to escape from a hunting dog. I dodged to the right to miss a small tree that suddenly appeared in front of my nose. The branch of a wait-a-bit thorn reached out and grasped my shirt. I twisted to pull myself free. I heard my shirt rip and could feel the tiny barbed thorns tearing into the flesh of my arm. I shook the thorn branch off and, frantically pushed my way through the bushes until I reached the path. I could see Kamau's back as he streaked away. I slowed and looked for the others. My heart thudded as I crouched behind a tree and peered into the bush. Jon sped by. Dave passed me next, his long legs hurtling him along. Then Matt stumbled into the path and together we started running.

We didn't stop until we reached our tree fort. Our pursuers hadn't chased us very far. I guess they just wanted to scare us off.

In the safety of our tree house, with the rope ladder pulled up, we discussed what we'd seen.

"What were they doing, Kamau?" I asked. "Can you explain it to us?"

Kamau crossed his arms on his chest and looked down. "I can't tell you anything about oathing," he said. So I told the others what I had heard from my dad. They listened closely.

Matt asked, "Do Christians take this oath?"

I looked at Kamau, but he was staring at the floor. "No," I answered. "The oath involves swearing by the traditional gods and spirits of the ancestors. My dad says a lot of Christians have been persecuted for refusing to take the oath."

"That's strange," said Matt, shaking his head. "Did you notice that man wearing a suit and tie in the group of oath-takers?"

"Yeah," I answered, "what about him?"

"Well," Matt said, "he looked a lot like one of the church leaders for this area. I went with my dad a few months ago to a church where he teaches Bible classes, and one of the preachers looked like that man. At least I think so. Oh, I don't know. Maybe I'm just imagining it. I'm sure a pastor wouldn't take the oath."

Kamau looked sick. "We shouldn't tell anyone what we saw," he advised.

We were all puzzled by our experience, but we agreed not to tell our parents. They might decide not to let us go down to our tree house in the forest anymore.

We headed home in the cool of the approaching night. We saw two pigeons, but we didn't even try to pot one. That's how much the experience had upset us.

By the next week we had pretty much forgotten the oathing incident. I rushed downstairs for breakfast. Taking my toast, I folded it and stuffed it into my mouth.

"Slow down, Dean," Mom said. "They won't leave for the Safari Rally without you."

I ignored her and stuffed two bananas into my pocket. She smiled and handed me a packed lunch. I jammed my green bush hat on my head, dashed out the door and sprinted for Matt's house. This was the day Matt's dad had promised to take the four of us to watch the Safari Rally. Each year this four-day car race attracted cars and drivers from all over the world. Unlike the Rhino Charge, this race was on roads, but they were some of the roughest roads in Africa. This was the first day of the race, and the cars would pass within ten miles of Rugendo.

We gathered at Matt's house. We all had our own packed lunches, and Mrs. Chadwick sent along a vacuum jug of iced tea. Kamau brought a flask of Kenyan chai. We had scorecards and a printed program telling the names of all the drivers, their numbers, and what kind of car they drove. Matt had his small radio turned on, but we couldn't hear much more than the roar of engines as the cars were flagged off the starting ramp at two-minute intervals from Kenyatta Conference Center in Nairobi. In an hour they would be driving by Rugendo.

Mr. Chadwick came out. We all jumped into the Land Rover. He reversed it out of the driveway, and we began bumping down the road. Mr. Chadwick leaned back and told us he'd found a good place to watch the cars. "I saw it last week when I was doing a leadership seminar at one of the churches. There's a hairpin curve with a giant hole in the middle. It rained this week so I think there'll be water in the hole. That should make the curve slick with mud. There's a place where we can park the Land Rover away from the road. We can climb above the curve and watch the cars. They'll have to go slowly, or they'll scrape bottom and skid off the road. And we'll be there to see it all."

"Sounds great," we all enthused from the back. Matt just grinned. I could tell he was proud of his dad.

"Will we be able to greet the drivers?" Kamau asked.

"We can wave at them," Dave answered, "but they'll be driving too fast to wave back at us."

"Wow, this is perfect," Jon shouted as we arrived at the spot. He scrambled up the hill. We followed and soon gathered at the top like a troop of baboons. We huddled around the radio, trying to hear the reports from Nairobi, but the steep mountains in the area made the reception fuzzy.

I heard the car first. "Here comes one," I said. "Can you hear it?" Matt turned off the radio, and we all listened. Sure enough, a throaty roar began to build to a crescendo. A rally car burst into view.

"Car number three. That's Bjorkman, the Swedish driver," I said, having already memorized the top drivers and their numbers.

Dave, our detail man, examined his scorecard and confirmed my identification. "Bjorkman started third, but he's already passed two cars. He must really be sailing. He'll bust his car long before the finish."

We all watched, transfixed, as Bjorkman went into a controlled skid around a bend in the road. He approached the hairpin curve beneath us. He hit the water hole at full speed. Water splashed into the air. The car started sliding on the glassy-slick mud.

"He's out of control," Matt murmured hoarsely.

"Will he crash?" Kamau asked, his hand ready to cover his eyes. It seemed to happen in slow motion. The car looked like it was floating off the road. We heard the harsh sound of branches breaking as it dipped into the ravine. As we watched, too astonished to move, both drivers emerged from where the car had stopped, listing at a steep angle like a sinking boat.

"Come on boys," Mr. Chadwick said. "Let's see if we can help."

Just then another rally car roared by. This one, driven by a local driver, slowed down at the curve before accelerating up the hill, spraying mud behind it.

Staying well off the road, we ran down to see if we could help Bjorkman. I watched his codriver, dressed in white coveralls, pull himself out from under the front of the car

"Anything broken?" Mr. Chadwick asked.

"It looks OK," the codriver answered in heavily accented English. "Just some bent bodywork. We were lucky not to hit any big trees. But we're really stuck in here, and I don't know how we'll get the car out."

The two Swedes shook their heads. "We're out of the race now," Bjorkman said. "And after so much practice and so much money to get here. What a waste."

"Why don't you use your winch to pull them out, Dad?" Matt asked. I wished I'd thought of the idea.

Bjorkman looked at us intently. "Do you really have a winch?"

"Yeah. My Land Rover's parked just up the hill," Mr. Chadwick said. "I've pulled cars out of worse situations than this. My guess is we'll have you back on the road in less than fifteen minutes. Will that keep you in the race?"

Bjorkman gave Mr. Chadwick an incredulous look. "You really have a Land Rover here? Go get it! I've already gained ten minutes. We'd only be five minutes behind."

We ran up the hill with Mr. Chadwick to get the Land Rover.

Another rally car roared by, flicking mud and stones in our direction. One rock stung me in the middle of my back, but I hardly noticed it. We were actually helping a rally driver! I couldn't wait to tell the other kids when school opened in three weeks.

Dave directed Mr. Chadwick carefully as he parked in front of Bjorkman's car in a place where he wouldn't obstruct any other rally cars driving past. Mr. Chadwick hopped out and began to play out the steel winch cable. Matt and I ran the end of the cable with its large curved hook over to Bjorkman's car. The drivers quickly attached it. Jon and Kamau threw an old blanket from the back of the Land Rover over the now taut cable. The blanket would keep the cable from killing anyone if it snapped. The winch growled softly as it slowly and steadily pulled the car until it bumped over the ridge and back onto the road.

Matt and I pulled the cable hook off while Bjorkman and his codriver made a quick check of the suspension. They jumped in and started the engine, which roared to life. The car's hood vibrated wildly on top of the pulsing engine. Bjorkman looked out and asked, "How can I thank you enough for your help?"

Mr. Chadwick smiled. "There's no need to thank us. We're Christians, and we follow what Jesus taught when he told us to help our neighbors in any way we can."

"Well," Bjorkman said reaching out his hand, "I do thank you. Very much." Mr. Chadwick gripped his hand firmly and shook it. "And thank you boys, too." Kamau stepped forward and shook Bjorkman's hand.

Determined to make up for lost time, Bjorkman released the clutch and raced up the hill, fishtailing in the mud.

"Boy, that was exciting!" Matt exclaimed. "Did you see inside the car? They had a roll bar and a Global Positioning System and all kinds of fancy equipment. Both drivers had helmets and ear-phones so they can talk to each other while they're driving."

"Yeah, that was great," Dave agreed. "The inside of that car had so many instruments it looked like the cockpit of an airplane." He started to identify all the things he'd seen using technical names.

None of the rest of us understood him, but we respected his knowledge.

Kamau smiled. "The driver was a good man. He greeted me."

"Is that all you can think of, Kamau?" I asked. "That Bjorkman shook your hand? Weren't you amazed that he slid off the road right in front of us so we'd have the chance to help him?"

"That was good," Kamau answered. "But it is very important in Kenya to greet someone when you meet them for the first time. And the driver took time to shake my hand."

More cars passed. "That's Patrick Njiru in car number 21," Dave pointed out as a Subaru motored past.

Kamau looked amazed. "A Kenyan drove that car?"

"Yeah," Dave explained. "Patrick Njiru is Kenya's number one rallying ace."

It wasn't as exciting anymore just watching the cars zoom past. I kept remembering what it was like actually talking to a driver, looking inside his car, and helping him.

"I think the Lord had Bjorkman slide off the road right where he did so we could help him and be an example of the love of Jesus," Mr. Chadwick said. The missionaries at Rugendo were al-ways saying things like that, but this time, we understood what he meant. We all felt pretty good when the last car whizzed past, and we clambered back into the Land Rover for the trip home.

"I'd like to be a rally driver," Jon said on the way home. "Wouldn't that be fun! Driving fast along these roads, doing controlled skids around the corners and stuff."

"I'd drive a Subaru Legacy," I said, gripping an imaginary steering wheel.

"I want to be like Patrick Njiru," Kamau said.

Matt scratched his chin. "We're not old enough to drive cars, but what if we had a bicycle safari? We could set up a route around Rugendo with a starting ramp, control points, and a finishing line. Our parents could help us with the timing, and we could have a race."

Like I said, Matt always comes up with ideas. That's why we made him our club captain.

"A bike race!" I said excitedly. "That would be great." The others began making plans.

"I'm going to ride so fast, I'll skid around the corners," Jon bragged.

"I'll borrow my father's big black Hero Jet bicycle," Kamau said.

"I could use the plywood from our packing crates and build a starting ramp just like the cars have in the real Safari Rally," Dave said. When we got home that afternoon, we were tired and muddy, but we had a story to tell our families about helping the Swedish drivers.

We could hardly wait for the next day when Matt had scheduled a meeting at our tree house to plan the bike safari.

CHAPTER THREE

PLANNING THE BIKE SAFARI

I arrived first at our tree house the next day. As the secretary, I had remembered to stuff a folded piece of paper and a pencil into my jeans pocket for taking notes at the meeting. I climbed the tree to where we had hidden our rope ladder in a hole. I pulled the rope ladder out and secured it to a large branch, climbed into the tree house and drew the ladder in after me.

I pulled out my paper and smoothed it on the rough board that served as my note-taking desk. The point of my pencil had broken off while I was running through the forest. I dug into my pocket for my Swiss army knife and, after choosing an appropriate blade, began whittling my pencil to a sharp point. Someone called from below.

"Who goes there?" I yelled.

"It's me. Jon," answered the voice below.

"Give the secret pass code," I instructed him.

"Rugendo Rhinos really rally behind rare rhinos," Jon said rapidly.

I threw down the ladder. I knew it was Jon all along, but Matt insisted we never let anyone up who didn't repeat the pass code. Pretty soon Dave, Matt, and Kamau showed up.

"The meeting will come to order," Matt announced. "We'll skip roll call because we know we're all here. Now our first and only item of business today is to organize this bike race. Agreed?"

"Agreed." We all nodded.

"First," Matt continued, "who gets to enter?"

"We do, of course," answered Jon.

"I know that," Matt answered. "But if we're the only ones who enter, we won't have much competition. I was thinking we could open the race up to any kids in the community as long as they have a bike to ride."

"Great idea," I said, making a note that the rally would be open to anyone with a bike.

"I think we should have an entry fee as well," Matt went on. "Of course, none of us would have to pay because we're organizing the race. But for the others, we should make them pay a fee, just like in the Safari Rally."

"Wait a minute," Kamau objected. "I don't think that's fair. I'm sure there'll be some kids who will want to join but won't have money for the entry fee. What do we need money for anyway?"

Matt scratched his head. He always did this when he was thinking. "Yeah," he said slowly, "we wouldn't want anyone left out because he couldn't pay. I'd feel like a mean old hyena if that happened. But we could use that money to buy a trophy for the winner. I saw some neat trophies at the Nairobi Sports House the last time I went there to get the puncture in my soccer ball fixed."

We all liked the idea of a trophy, but we didn't want to leave anyone out. I suggested we have a fifty-shilling entry fee, but that we make it optional. When a person entered, we would explain to him the money would be used to buy a trophy. If a person couldn't pay, he could still enter, but the more people who paid, the better the trophy would be.

With that agreed, Dave said his dad would help build a starting ramp and a finishing ramp just like the Safari Rally cars had in Nairobi.

"Now we're getting somewhere," Jon said enthusiastically. "Man! Real ramps!"

The meeting went on most of the morning. We decided to have a secret drawing of numbers from a hat right before the bike rally. The riders would leave at one-minute intervals. Dave volunteered his dad to time the finish.

"Looks like all that's left is to map out the race course," I said, surveying the list of items I had written down. Right away everyone had his own idea of where the race should go.

"We should start down by the old cemetery," Jon began.

Dave interrupted him. "No, I say we start in front of my house because—" He never got a chance to finish his sentence.

Matt stood to his feet shouting, "Order! Order!" We got quiet in a hurry and listened to our leader. "This is what we'll do," Matt said. "This afternoon we'll meet at the soccer field on our bikes. We'll drive over every inch of road on the mission station. We'll do it together. But, as you can see, the final decision can't be made by a committee." Looking at me, he asked, "Tell me, Dean, when they map out the route for the Safari Rally, how many people do it?"

I knew the answer because each year I studied the souvenir

program I bought for watching the Safari cars. "It's one man," I said. "He drives all over Kenya deciding which roads the cars will use. Sometimes he has a companion on his trips, but the decision is made by one man."

I felt a bit disappointed. I knew what Matt was driving at. If we tried to make the decision as a club, we'd just squabble. We'd already demonstrated that. Now Matt would decide on the route himself.

"Right," Matt said after hearing my answer. "So we'll ride the roads together. Each person can point out what he likes about certain parts of the roads. But the final decision will be made by," he paused for emphasis, "Dean."

"By me?" I could hardly believe what I'd just heard. "Why me, Matt? You're the club captain."

"Yeah, I'm the captain, but you're the guy who spends all that time studying the real Safari. I think you'd do the best job of setting up a route for our bike safari."

The meeting dismissed, and we climbed down and hid the rope ladder as usual. I was elated by the job I'd been given.

Far away in the woods we heard the harsh, nasal cry of a blue monkey. Actually blue monkeys were a dark greenish gray with a white collar. They traveled in troops along the treetops eating leaves and fruit and raiding the corn *shambas* or farms in the area. Normally we would have tracked the monkeys down. But today we wanted to get home for lunch so we could spend the afternoon checking out the roads we would use for the bike safari.

When we reached Rugendo, a herd of sheep and goats blocked the road. "It's my younger brother, Chege," said Kamau. Chege came over and talked with Kamau. "I'm sorry," Kamau said to us.

"I won't be able to ride with you and decide where the race will go. My father says I have to help Chege watch over our flock this afternoon. I don't care where the race goes. I'll ride fast on whatever roads you choose." We waved good-bye as Kamau and Chege led their sheep and goats toward some green grass.

When I got home I took out a large sheet of paper and sketched a map of the whole station so I could write notes on it during the afternoon. In the evening I could finalize the route.

At lunch my mother scolded me for eating so fast. I told my parents about our plan for the bike safari and how we were going out after lunch to discuss the route. I also asked my dad if he could do the timing at the start of the race. He smiled and said he'd be glad to.

"That's good, because I already told the guys you would. Well, good-bye Mom, Dad. I have to meet the other Rhinos at the soccer field."

"Wait just a minute, young man," Mom said. "Are you forgetting that you wash lunch dishes?"

"Oh yeah. I did forget, Mom. Honest." I set down my map and started running the hot water for dishes.

"What's this?" Dad asked, picking up the map I'd drawn.

"Oh, it's just a map of the station," I answered. "I drew it so I could make notes this afternoon. We're all going to ride around, but Matt says I get to make the final decision on the actual route for our race."

"That's great," Dad said. "I'm really proud of you, Dean." His eyes narrowed as he scanned the map I'd drawn. I turned and started washing the dishes.

"This map," Dad said slowly after he'd studied it.

27

I got embarrassed. "I know it's not very good," I started.

He stopped me. "No, it's very detailed. I like it. But there's a road I don't think you know about. It would be an ideal place for part of your bike race."

A road I didn't know about? How could it be? We Rhinos thought we'd explored every inch of Rugendo and the surrounding woods on our hunts. "Where is this road, Dad?" I asked, putting down the dish rag.

"Come over here to the table," he said. Then, spreading the map out, he pointed to a place just east of the station. "In the 1800s Rugendo was a camp for Arab slave traders. Here they would gather slaves from all over this area. When they had enough, they would head for the coast. The slave caravan path grew into a fair-sized road. It's not used anymore, but it's still enough of a path for your bikes. The road goes right along here." He took his pen and drew the road onto my map.

"When the mission started here in the early 1900s, the first missionaries came in on that slave road. But with the coming of the railroad, a new road was built to the south to link up with the nearest railroad station. Since then all traffic has gone out on the present main road over here." He pointed it out on the map, and I nodded.

"But how did you know about the old slave caravan road?" I asked.

"That's another long story," Dad said with a laugh. "To make it short, an old Kikuyu man whose father told him stories about escaping a slave raid on his village told me about it. When I was skeptical, he offered to show me the place. I went with him and saw it several years ago. It's a bit overgrown, but the base of the

28

old slave road is very smooth, and it would be excellent for riding bikes on."

I shook my head in amazement. "A real slave caravan road. Won't the other guys be surprised! Thanks, Dad. This will make our bike safari really exciting."

I headed for the door and my bike.

"Wait a minute, Dean," Dad said.

I turned, expecting some other information on the slave road. Instead he pointed at the sink. "Dishes, remember?"

"Oh yeah," I answered. "Dishes."

CHAPTER FOUR

PLOTTING THE RACE ROUTE

"**S**orry I'm late," I apologized to the others as I skidded my bike to a stop by the soccer field.

"It's about time, Dean," Matt snapped. "We've been waiting for at least ten minutes. What kept you?"

I shrugged and tried to hide my prune-wrinkled dishwater hands. I took out my map and spread it on the ground. "Here's a map I made of the station," I said lamely, hoping Matt would think I was late because I was finishing the map. "You can lead the way, Matt." Again, I was trying to appease Matt and keep him from the topic of why I had been late. No one else ever had to wash dishes. Their parents had house help to do those kinds of chores. But my mom always said she didn't need house help when she had kids like me. My smoke screen worked. Matt started to push off on his new ten-speed bike.

"You guys can give me your ideas as we ride around. I'll take notes of what you say. Tonight I'll use everyone's ideas to draw the final route map." By the end I was shouting to make sure I could be heard. I'm not sure Matt heard, but Jon and Dave nodded as they pedaled away.

Matt headed straight for hospital hill. It was a steep hill that went from the church down to the mission hospital. I secretly called it dead man's hill. And not only because the old mission cemetery stood at the bottom. I still remembered riding my tricycle down the hill when I was only four. The front wheel twirled faster and faster pushing my feet off the pedals. And on that trike, back-pedaling was the only means of braking. Unable to stop, I headed my little blue trike into the ditch and had a tremendous crash, flying over the handlebars and landing in the grass. To this day my stomach flipped as if I'd eaten a whole pan of flying ants live, wings and all, whenever I had to ride down that hill.

Matt braked to a stop at the top of hospital hill. "Get this down, Dean," he said as I pulled up. "This hill would be a great stretch for our bike safari. We can really cruise here."

I gulped and hoped no one else noticed. "Actually I'd hoped to route the safari up this hill," I said trying to keep the tremble out of my voice.

"Up! Never! It's too steep," Matt scoffed. "We'd all have to get off our bikes and push. Nahh! It's got to be downhill." With a whoop he started straight down followed by Jon.

Dave paused and looked at me. "Are you okay, Dean?"

I nodded and took a deep breath. I took my bush hat off and wiped the sweat off my forehead with the brim of the hat. I followed Dave down the hill, squeezing tightly to my brake handles and praying they wouldn't be worn down to the metal. I managed to reach the bottom without making it plain to the rest how scared I was.

We kept pedaling around the station, stopping every so often to make comments. I jotted down notes. At about 5:30 P.M. we

31

pulled up again at the soccer field after exploring all the roads of Rugendo.

"Well, that's it," Matt said. "It's up to you now, Dean, to make the final decisions." He paused, then added, "But we'd better go down hospital hill, not up."

I smiled tightly. "You bet, Matt, but we have one more road to check out."

"What do you mean, one more road?" asked Dave. "We've been on every road there is! And my legs are tired enough to prove it!"

I pulled out the map and told them my dad's story about the old slave road. They all wanted to see it.

"It'll be dark in about an hour," Matt said, "but we'll have time to see if this road is good enough for riding bikes. Imagine! An old slave trade road right here at Rugendo!"

I led the way. We passed the local primary school and saw some old ruined buildings. "My dad said these houses were the first ones the missionaries lived in when they came here," I commented.

"We knew about these old houses," answered Matt. "We just never knew about the slave road."

We passed the houses and rode into the trace of an old path through a thicket of large trees.

"Right through here," I said dodging between two pencil cedar trees. The late afternoon sun didn't penetrate into the forest, and it was dark.

"Kind of spooky," Jon said. He was usually a brave adventurer, but at ten years old he was the youngest in our group and darkness wasn't much of an adventure for him.

"It's just on the other side here, according to my dad," I said, trying to sound encouraging. I felt a bit scared myself. It was now after 6 P.M. and darkness falls quickly at the equator. I recognized a large boulder that my dad had described as being the entrance to the road. "There it is," I cried, pointing.

The trees thinned and the lingering rays of sunshine made it easier to see. "Pretty firm," Dave remarked, getting off his bike and walking on the path. He looked almost like his dad testing a riverbed before attempting to cross. "Yes," Dave approved, "we could ride pretty fast on this."

Matt loved it. "This is great! We could start the race up here at the top. Wouldn't that be something? Holding our bike safari on an old slave road."

Seeing the other guys excited made me happy, too. This had been a great idea. My dad was quite a guy.

We kept riding. After about a quarter of a mile, we came to a rockslide, covering the trail. "Looks like this is where we'll have to start our race," I said. "We can't ride our bikes any further back up in here."

"It'll be great," Jon said. We sat there for a few minutes, delighted with the idea of revealing the old slave road to all the other kids who would enter the race.

Matt got up. "We'd better go," he said looking at his watch. "It'll be dark soon."

"Yeah, let's go," I said. "I'm glad you like this old road. I'm not sure of the whole route yet, but this will definitely be the starting section."

"And we'll ride down hospital hill," Matt reminded me.

"Sure, Matt," I said, hoping he didn't notice my lack of enthusiasm.

We rode down the gentle slope. Just before the thicket of trees there was a sharp hairpin bend that turned right and then left to avoid a deep ravine. The ravine was choked with vines, ferns, and stinging nettles. "This curve will be a thriller," Jon said, riding beside me. "We'll have to see how fast we can go without losing control and skidding into the ravine. Boy, it's deep down there," he peered into the threatening gully.

I nodded and gripped my brakes more tightly.

We were in the middle of the thicket when the sun dropped. We could almost feel it get darker. That's how night comes in Kenya. Within five or ten minutes it would be completely dark.

The path through the trees was narrow. "Don't worry, we're almost home," Matt assured us. The tone of his voice was not as confident as his words. I could tell he was worried. We sped through the trees.

I spotted the man first. "Look over there," I shouted. "Someone is watching us!"

Dave ran his bike into the back of mine as I braked, and we both fell into the green undergrowth.

"Ouch!" Dave screamed. "Stinging nettles!" I had fallen on one arm, and brushed against a stinging nettle, too. The plants grew thick in the highland forests of Kenya. They didn't do any permanent damage, but they stung like fire if you touched one.

"What is your problem?" Matt asked, irritated. "First someone's watching us, and now stinging nettles are after us. Come on, stop holding us back."

"I really saw a man," I said, defending myself. "He was running along parallel to us and staring right at you, Matt."

"Why would someone stare at us?" Matt asked. "I think you just saw a shadow. Or maybe a blue monkey. Come on. Let's get moving. This place is giving me the creeps."

We all agreed. We shot out of the woods and sped down the road to our homes. I knew I hadn't just seen a shadow. It had been a man. And his face was familiar, but I couldn't remember where I'd seen it.

We got to Jon's house first. He waved and pulled into his driveway. Dave peeled off next. Matt's house was next to mine. We said good-bye as the dregs of the day's sunlight dropped behind the volcanic mountains to the west leaving a ribbon of orange and red. My dad was probably taking another photograph of yet another breathtaking sunset.

I felt tired, and my mind puzzled over the man I'd seen in the woods. Finally I put it out of my head. After supper I laid out the final route for our bike safari with the start at the rockslide on the old slave trail. I even included a section going down hospital hill. I made a mental note to check my brakes.

I drew a detailed map and got permission from my dad to make copies on the photocopy machine at his office in the morning. Then I went to bed.

The next day I ran off copies and took the maps to Matt's house. We picked up Dave, Jon, and Kamau and began recruiting riders for our bike safari. We went to the homes of the missionaries on the station and got four other guys who wanted to ride. Then we faced a problem. A big problem.

CHAPTER FIVE

A CASE OF
MISTAKEN IDENTITY?

We rounded the corner where Rugendo's towering steel water tank glistened in the sun. Jill and her Cheetah club stood astride their bikes forming a roadblock. We skidded to a stop and faced Jill, Rachel, Rebekah, and Freddie.

"We hear you're organizing a bike safari," Jill said, the breeze blowing her honey-colored hair across her face. She let go of her handlebar to push her hair back. Jill Artberry, whose parents produced Christian radio programs, had started the Cheetahs club to find out who'd been behind the carjackings at Rugendo in a previous adventure.

"Yes, we are," Matt replied cautiously, "but I don't see how that news would affect you girls. Now could you move out of the way? We're busy organizing the race." Matt started to ride his bike through a gap between the girls' bikes.

The girls closed the gap.

"We want to race," Rachel said, pushing her bike forward. Her bike helmet tilted to the left. Rachel's gaze swept over the whole group of girls. "All of us."

Rachel and Rebekah Maxwell's parents had recently moved out of Zaire because of war in that country, and their parents now worked in Nairobi, waiting to see what would happen in Zaire, which had already changed its name to Congo. The girls had come out to stay with Jill for a few weeks during school vacation.

Freddie, leaning her red bike a little too far to the left as she stood in the line, suddenly toppled over. She jumped to her feet and brushed the dirt off her jeans, which had holes in the knees.

"Yeah, we want to ride in the race," Freddie said. Freddie normally went home to Uganda during our school break, but her mother was going to have a baby any day. Her family had come to stay in the mission guest house across the road from the Rugendo Hospital.

"We probably have room for more riders," I said, trying to appease the girls.

"What are you doing, Dean?" Matt cut in. "You can't expect the Cheetahs to join in! We're not having any girls in this race! Our bike safari is for boys only. It's going to be too tough for girls to keep up."

"We heard what you said to the other guys you asked to join the race," Jill argued. "You said anyone who had a bike could enter. We have bikes, and we want to enter. I don't see why we can't. I'm faster than most of you guys anyway. I bet that's why you won't let us race. You're afraid you might get beat by a girl."

"We're not afraid of any girls, that's for sure," Matt said. "Give us a chance to talk about this, OK, Jill?" Matt said. "We'll let you know later."

Jill looked at her watch. "OK, we'll give you Rhinos one hour to decide. And if you don't let us race, we'll tell our parents that you boys left us out." The Cheetahs pulled their bikes aside and rode away.

"Whew! Now what do we do?" Matt asked. "I sure don't want any girls in the race. Beat us? Ha! If they're part of the bike safari, they'll never make it over some of those hills Dean put in the route."

"Tell her they can't race," Jon said firmly. "Girls will just get in the way. We're the organizers. If we say boys only, then it's boys only."

"Girls shouldn't be in a boys' bike race," Kamau agreed.

"But we said anyone with a bike," I put in. "We can't go back on that or make up new rules now. I never thought girls would want to race in our bike safari, or I'd have made a rule to say any *boy* with a bike could enter."

"We can change the rules if we want," Matt said. "It's our race." He paused. "But if we don't let them race, the girls will say we're afraid to race against them."

We sat silently. I didn't see any reason why Jill and the Cheetahs shouldn't be allowed to ride in the race, but I couldn't say that openly or the other Rhinos would accuse me of liking a girl. Matt hurled a rock at a nearby tree, and it smacked the trunk with a loud thwack.

I had an idea. "We're sort of copying the Safari Rally with our bike race, aren't we?" I began slowly.

Everyone agreed.

"Well, sometimes ladies drive in the Safari Rally," I said. "In fact, in 1963 when only seven cars finished the race because of floods, one of the seven finishing cars was driven by two ladies.

The Safari Rally even awards a special trophy to the highest placing women drivers. So if the Safari Rally has women drivers, we could, too. I mean, if you all agree."

Matt nodded his head slowly. He looked at Kamau, Dave, and Jon. "What do you guys think?"

"It doesn't seem right for boys and girls to race against each other," Kamau said. "But I'm not afraid to race against them."

Dave spoke grudgingly. "I guess it's OK as long as you're sure ladies drive in the real Safari."

"It's true," I assured him and offered to show him the story of the Magnificent Seven of 1963 in my official history book of the Safari Rally.

Jon agreed, too. "OK," he said, "let the Cheetahs race. But let's beat them so badly they won't ever want to race against boys again."

We went to Jill's house and told the Cheetahs we'd decided they could enter. Jill's smile lit up her face. The Cheetahs even paid double the entry fee when they heard the money would be spent on a trophy for the winner. "We don't mind spending extra to help buy a nice trophy since the trophy will sit in our clubhouse, anyway," Jill said confidently.

Matt turned and jumped on his bike. We followed and could hear him muttering under his breath, "She makes my blood boil!"

At the end of the day we had fourteen riders entered in the Rugendo Rhinos Bicycle Safari. We had the five of us, four other guys from the mission station, Ben, the pastor's son, and the four Cheetahs. All the riders had a copy of the map, and we gave them three days to practice riding the course, which covered a distance of almost three miles. Since it was school vacation, we set the race for the next Tuesday morning at 10:00.

In the meantime, we Rhinos went to work helping cut the boards for the ramps with Dave's dad. We also had to recruit parents to man checkpoints at designated spots on the route so no one could cheat by taking a shortcut. Matt went to Nairobi with his dad to buy a trophy for the winner. He got one at Nairobi Sports House with a gold-colored bicycle rider mounted on a wooden stand.

The Sunday before the race, we all attended the Rugendo church as usual. I always had to sit with my parents. Matt, Dave, and Jon sat by themselves in a different row from their families. Sometimes I envied them, but my mom always said we should sit together as a family. Kamau came in late and sat next to me.

I looked up at the pulpit. Benjamin's dad, Pastor Kariuki, introduced a guest speaker from a nearby district. With a smile, Pastor Kariuki said the speaker was not only a good friend and brother in the Lord, but also his cousin.

After the introduction, the speaker stood up. I almost jumped out of my seat when I saw him. I sat straight up, straining to get a better view. I couldn't believe it! He looked exactly like the well-dressed man we'd seen at the oathing ceremony. Matt had said the man at the oathing ceremony resembled a church leader his father had taught. Could this be the same man?

I didn't hear much of the sermon, even though it was translated into English from Kikuyu for our benefit. My mind went back to the clearing where I'd seen the old *mundu mugo* oathing people. The picture played like a videotape in my mind. This man had been the one at the oathing ceremony. I was sure of it!

I had a feeling I'd seen him somewhere else, too. Maybe preaching at the church last year? I didn't know. The image of his face at the oathing ceremony made it impossible for me to concentrate on where else I may have seen him.

After church I asked Kamau if he thought the preacher was the well-dressed man we saw at the oathing ceremony.

He shook his head. "When I realized it was an oathing ceremony, I closed my eyes so I didn't see anyone besides the *mundu mugo*. But pastors don't take those oaths."

"You're right," I answered and strolled home. But the pastor's face kept nagging at my memory. While my mom finished putting dinner together, my dad and I set the table. "Don't forget to use our Sunday silver," Mom called. I pulled the box of fancy silverware from under the corner cupboard and arranged them by the china plates with maroon flowers on the edges that my dad had set.

"Dad," I asked, "do you know the guy who preached today?"

"You mean Reverend Kimani? Yes, I know him," Dad answered. "He's one of the strongest Kikuyu Christian leaders in the area. Why do you want to know?"

"Well, it's just that I think we saw him a week or so ago while we were hunting pigeons," I said. "And we saw him taking an oath in a secret ceremony led by a Kikuyu witch doctor."

"What are you talking about?" Dad asked.

I explained to him how we'd been hunting and had stumbled onto the ceremony. "And one of the men standing there taking the oath was the man who preached in church today," I finished.

My dad frowned. "I hadn't realized they were oathing so close to Rugendo," he said. "This oathing business is really serious, Dean. You and your friends had better stay closer to home on your hunts. No telling what would have happened to you if you'd been caught down there. I really don't think anyone would hurt you, but these oaths of loyalty to the tribe and clan are very strong. People who've taken the oath will do exactly as they're told."

"But why was Reverend Kimani taking that oath if he is a Christian?" I asked. "You told me Christians were resisting the oath and even being persecuted for their stand against oathing."

My dad laughed gently. "I'm convinced you saw an oathing ceremony in the woods," he said. "But I'm also convinced you did not see Reverend Kimani there. Like you said, the Christians have been resisting the oath-taking. And one of the most vocal leaders encouraging Christians to resist the oath is Reverend Kimani. He even wrote an article for our magazine urging Christians to stand firm against this oathing business."

"But we saw him!" I insisted. "And he took the oath."

"Dean, I think you saw a man who may have looked like him, but I'm sure you didn't see Reverend Kimani," Dad answered. "You know how so many Kikuyu people look similar to us. It's kind of funny. The other day I was talking to an old Kikuyu man. I introduced him to some of the other missionaries at the office. He said he couldn't tell missionaries apart because all white people looked the same to him!" Dad laughed.

I laughed with him. I saw his point, but I'd been so sure.

"So you think we really didn't see Reverend Kimani at the oathing ceremony, but someone who looked like him?" I asked.

Dad put an arm on my shoulder. "Yes, I think it's just a case of mistaken identity, Dean."

Mom called us to dinner, and we sat down to a warthog roast with mashed potatoes and gravy and sweet Kenya-highland-grown carrots. What a meal! The meat was tender and juicy. Dad had shot the warthog on a hunting trip the month before, and we'd stocked our freezer with meat. It tasted so good it made me forget my suspicions about Reverend Kimani and the oath-taking ceremony we Rhinos had seen.

THE RACE

I woke shortly before 6 A.M. I could hear the birds singing in the bottlebrush tree outside my window. I jumped out of bed and started to get dressed. This was the day of our bike safari! All the preparations had been made. The race would start at 10:00 A.M. sharp. Only four hours from now! I had been practicing riding my bike over the route for the past week. I knew I had a good chance of winning, as I was one of the biggest guys in the race and could beat anyone going uphill. I still wouldn't admit to my fellow Rhinos that I was afraid to go downhill at high speed. I had worn my brakes down almost to the metal. Matt would be my main competition because he loved flying downhill. His brakes still had rubber nubs on them as if they'd never been used. Before going downstairs I said a brief prayer and asked God to help me overcome my fear of going downhill.

In the kitchen I poured myself a bowl of cereal and made some toast. Dad came in to perk his coffee. "Up pretty early, aren't you?" he asked, rubbing his eyes. What hair he had left on the sides of his balding head stood up on end like the wind-ruffled mane of a lion.

"Today's the bike safari, Dad," I answered.

He smiled. "I know, I'm the timer, remember? But I would have thought you could have used some extra rest. After all, the race doesn't start until 10:00."

I shrugged. "I couldn't sleep. Anyway, I have to help set up the starting ramp."

Dad put his hand on my shoulder. "You're excited and that's good. Save up some of that energy for the race and you'll win for sure."

After breakfast I went over to Matt's house. I threw a small rock that clacked against his window. No answer. I threw a handful of pebbles. Matt's window opened. "What is it?" he asked, still half-asleep.

"Safari day," I said. "We have to get the ramps set up and make sure all the parents know where to go."

"What time is it, anyway?" Matt muttered, looking at his watch. "It's not even 7:00. Dean, you're a fanatic!"

He got up and in a few minutes he opened the door still grumbling at the early hour. I sat at the table while he had some eggs for breakfast. His mom asked us which checkpoint she was supposed to run. We tried to explain it to her, but she got mixed up. So after breakfast we had her drive the car to where we wanted her to stand and explained again what she was supposed to do.

By now Jon joined us. We made sure all the other parents knew where to be and what to do. We thought we'd made it clear before, but if Matt's mom was confused, others might be as well. We thought we'd better make sure.

When we finished, we went to Dave's house. Kamau and Dave stood in the driveway handing tools to their dads as they helped

Mr. Krenden build the finishing ramp. Kamau's dad handed a nail to Kamau and pointed at a two-by-four. Kamau nodded and hammered the nail into the boards. His dad watched him proudly.

Mr. Krenden announced, "Well, boys, it's done. What do you think?"

"It's great!" Matt spoke for all of us. We had chosen Dave's driveway for the finish since it was in the middle of the mission station. Dave's dad had the starting ramp all ready to go in the back of his pickup truck. We put our bikes in the pickup and drove as near to the starting point on the old slave trail as we could get.

We carried the pieces of the starting ramp the rest of the way and Dave and Kamau helped Mr. Krenden set it up. We waited for the other riders to arrive. I had brought my canteen along. I knew the weight might slow me up a bit, but the water would taste good at the checkpoints. I pulled out the canteen and took a swig, wiped the neck, and passed it around to the others.

Shortly after 9:30 most of the riders had arrived, including Jill's gang. Jill's aqua-blue mountain bike gleamed in the early morning sun as she got off and flicked down the kickstand with her foot.

"We're ready!" she announced. She even had riding gloves with padding in the palms to reduce the impact when she rode over bumps. Her shoulder length hair spilled out behind her dark blue riding helmet. All the Cheetahs had helmets.

Matt nodded toward them and gave a curt greeting. "Get ready for the draw," Matt ordered.

Everyone gathered around, and Matt pulled out numbers one through four so the younger kids in the race could choose them and be the first riders off the ramp.

"Who's got a hat?" Matt asked.

As usual, I was wearing my bush hat made of thick green khaki which had two small round holes on each side covered with thin mesh-wire screens. This kept my head cool inside the hat. I wore my hat so often it had begun to fray at the edges. Sometimes I even wore it to bed. One side of the hat's brim stood up against the side of my head while the other side flopped down. A shimmering red and blue turaco feather peeked out of a small pocket on one side.

"Use mine," I offered.

Rebekah complained, "His hat is ragged and smelly. Use my bike helmet instead."

Matt scowled slightly. "A helmet is not a hat" he said. We'll put the numbers into Dean's bush hat."

We had four nine-year-olds, so Matt tossed the numbers one through four into the bush hat and shook them up. Holding the hat above his head, Matt told the nine-year-olds to choose their numbers. Then the rest of the numbers were thrown into the hat.

"Girls choose first," Rachel told Matt as he shook the numbers around.

Matt rolled his eyes. "Of course you girls can choose first," he said.

Jill pulled out a number. "Seven," she said. "The perfect number in the Bible. I'm sure that means I'll have a perfect race."

"We'll see about that," Matt muttered.

Kamau drew number five. He smiled. "You'll have a hard time passing me on my big bike," he said.

I drew number fourteen, the last rider to start. Matt started just before me at number thirteen. We had debated whether to leave the number thirteen out of the race. The real Safari Rally never had number thirteen, thinking it was unlucky. They went from number twelve to fourteen, but we'd decided that as Christians we shouldn't be superstitious. So we had a number thirteen. And Matt picked it.

After we had chosen our numbers, Dave said, "I have a surprise." He pulled out a large brown envelope. He shook it and round pieces of cardboard fluttered to the ground. The numbers one to fourteen had been carefully drawn on the pieces of cardboard. Each number had a loop of string attached. "Find your number and then hang it around your neck," Dave instructed. "That way people who are watching the race will know your number and how many people you've passed."

"Or how many have passed you," Matt said, his voice cocky.

My dad arrived with his stopwatch and at precisely 10 A.M. the first rider rolled down the ramp and pedaled furiously along the trail. We had planned a staggered start, just like the real Safari Rally, so every minute another rider took off. Kamau perched on top of his dad's tall black bike like a rider on a camel. When his time came to start, he pumped his legs up and down like pistons to get the big bike rolling.

Jill and her Cheetahs looked like long-legged beetles with their shiny helmets as they disappeared down and around the bend in the road.

Finally only Matt and I were left. "This is it, Dean," Matt said to me. "Good luck." With that he pushed his bike onto the ramp. His eyes narrowed to slits, and he grinned at me and gave me the thumbs-up signal.

My dad gave the final countdown. "Three, two, one, go!" Matt flew down the ramp. I shook my head. I would be lucky if I could catch up with him, but I knew I had to try. That's one thing my parents taught me: Keep trying right up to the end.

At last it was my turn. Just before I pushed off I caught a glimpse of Matt's back far ahead to the right before a sharp turn around the ravine. I pedaled hard to catch up. At the ravine corner I did a controlled skid, expecting to see Matt near the bottom of the long hill that led back to the station, but I couldn't see him anywhere. *He must have taken off at laser speed.*

The hill after the ravine was so steep I felt as if I was driving down a cliff. My hands began to grip my brakes. *No! I have to ride flat out or I'll never catch Matt,* I told myself. *That's why I can't see him. He's gone down the hill at full speed.*

Breathing a prayer to the Lord to keep me safe, I released my grip on the brakes and kept pedaling. My bike went faster and faster, but this time I was determined not to slow down. Maybe I shouldn't have been so determined.

At the bottom of the hill the road turned sharply to the right. I rode into the curve too fast and my bike slid sideways from underneath me. Dirt and rocks tore chunks of skin from my leg. Choking back tears, I remounted and pushed off again.

Only a few seconds lost in my fall, and I'm sure I've gained time on Matt, I told myself. I'd never gone down a hill so fast in my life. It felt great. I thanked the Lord for answering my prayer.

Soon I saw another rider, but it wasn't Matt. I passed, giving the thumbs-up sign as I sped by. I could see Kamau and others ahead, but not Matt. *This is really strange,* I thought. I wondered if he had somehow put a motorcycle engine on his bike. I laughed at the thought and began pushing myself even harder. I passed a few more riders.

I wrote my name in at each checkpoint, but I was in such a hurry I forgot to look for Matt's name. I knew he was ahead of me, and I wanted to catch him, but I never did. I steamed up the final hill, and I could hear people cheering. Some others had already finished the race, but the winner would be the one who had completed the course in the fastest time based on his or her starting time. Since I had started last, my time had to be better than everyone I'd passed. And the timer shouted out that my time was the best of those who had finished. I had won the Rugendo Rhinos Bicycle Safari! I felt great. I must have beaten Matt's time by just a few seconds.

"Great riding, Dean," Kamau said, shaking my hand.

"Where's Matt?" I asked after the joy of winning had settled in.

"He's not in yet," said Jon. "You must have really been flying to pass him. You know what a daredevil rider he is!"

"Not in? Are you sure, Jon?" I asked. "He started in front of me, and I never passed him. I chased him the whole race. That's why I rode so fast. How can he not be in?"

Kamau and Dave looked at each other. "I never saw Matt," Dave said.

"Me neither," Kamau said. We checked with Dave's dad who had timed the finish. He confirmed that Matt hadn't come in. Where was he?

We began asking the other riders. No one had seen Matt pass them during the race. By now all the other riders had finished—except Matt. We began to get worried. We forgot the presentation of the trophy and the iced tea and cookies. Something had happened to Matt!

"Matt has disappeared!" I called out to my dad. He grabbed

the papers that had been brought in from the checkpoints. Matt had not signed in at any of the checkpoints! Soon everyone gathered around trying to decide what to do.

"The last place I saw Matt was going into the ravine corner on the old slave road," I said.

"That's the best place to start looking," said my dad. "There's a steep drop-off there. Maybe Matt went over the edge."

"Knowing the way Matt rides his bike, I wouldn't be surprised," Matt's dad said grimly. "But before we search, let's pray."

After praying we Rhinos jumped into Mr. Chadwick's Land Rover to look for Matt. The Cheetahs jumped in after us. I suddenly remembered Matt's number in the race. Thirteen! Maybe it really was unlucky. I shivered. It felt like a hairy caterpillar was walking down the middle of my back again.

CHAPTER SEVEN

SEARCHING FOR MATT

When we reached the corner by the ravine, we jumped out and began searching. "Matt, Matt!" we called, but the trees and leaves in the forest swallowed the sound, and our only answer was an eerie silence.

We looked around the edge of the ravine. I ended up next to Jill. We gazed down a sharp fifteen-foot drop with some rocks at the bottom. "If Matt fell down here without a bike helmet on, he would have cracked his head open," Jill commented. None of us Rhinos liked to wear bike helmets, but I could see Jill's point.

Jon, with his excellent tracking abilities, discovered the first clue. "Over here!" he called. "The grass has been trampled, and there are crushed leaves on these bushes. This must be where Matt went over the edge."

We hurried to where Jon peered down into the thick growth in the ravine, and we called for Matt again. But once more we received no answer.

Matt's dad shook his head. "I can't figure it out. If Matt had skidded into the ravine, he should have fallen in over there, where his speed would have been the greatest. If he'd made it around the curve, his speed by this point would have been rather slow. It just doesn't make sense that he fell over the edge here."

We began climbing down the steep side of the ravine. We tried to avoid the stinging nettles, but there were too many. I had shorts on and soon my legs felt like they had an electric current surging down the skin from the powerful stings, but I kept on, desperately searching for Matt.

Jon led the way with my dad and Mr. Chadwick. They knew he had a knack for following a trail, and they used his skills wisely.

Halfway down the slope he stopped and pointed to something. We gathered around. "His bike was here all right," he said, pointing out some skid tracks that could have come from Matt's bike tires. "But he must have carried it from here, because there are no more bike tracks after this. There are footprints, but they go further down into the ravine."

I couldn't figure out what was going on. If Matt had fallen into the ravine and hadn't hit his head, he certainly would have pushed his bike back up the hill. Or at least crawled up the hill and called for help. Or stopped me as I rode by. But to carry his bike and go deeper into the ravine? It didn't make sense to me.

"Dear God, help us to find out what's happened to Matt," I prayed in my heart.

Everyone stopped again. Kamau stood next to me, a worried frown wrinkling his forehead. We had come to a rocky section where a river had once flowed. Kamau knelt down. "I don't see any more tracks," he said. The narrow ravine we'd been following began to flatten out, and there were several directions we could search.

My dad and Matt's dad looked at each other. "Where do we go from here?" Dad asked.

Matt's dad slumped down on a chair-sized rock. He shook his head. "I don't know," he answered. He took a deep breath. "Let's pray."

We huddled around as they asked God to show us the right direction. After praying, I had an idea. "Maybe one of us can climb a tree and try to see which way to go. I saw it work once in a movie." The others looked at me strangely. I shrugged. "Well, I thought it was at least worth a try."

Freddie believed in me. Maybe it was because she loved climbing trees. She had already scrambled up a Cape chestnut. It had very few branches at the bottom, but Freddie could shinny up a tree like a monkey. Near the top she stopped climbing and looked around the area. "Over there!" she shouted, pointing eagerly. "I see a small spring of water in that direction, and I think the mud around the spring has been churned up. Maybe it's Matt's footprints!"

Mr. Chadwick and my dad decided it was as good a direction as any, so they led us toward the spring as Freddie slid down the tree. We Rhinos followed our dads, while the Cheetahs brought up the rear. Arriving at the spring, we did find footprints. And we saw bike tracks, but something was very wrong. This time Dave noticed it first. "There are two sets of footprints here," he said. "And these other footprints look like they belong to a grown man." It seemed that Matt and whoever was with him had stopped for a drink. And then they had left, leaving no tracks on the rocks surrounding the spring. This time there were no tall trees to climb. It seemed we had reached the end of the trail.

In frustration I picked up a rock and hurled it into the bushes. To my surprise, I heard the clink of rock on metal. At first I thought my rock must have hit another rock.

"What was that noise?" Kamau asked.

"I don't know," I answered. "Let's go find out."

"Come back, Dean," my father called as Kamau and I began to run toward the bushes. "We have to stay together as a group. One lost boy is enough for one day."

"But Dad," I protested, "I threw a rock in there, and it hit something metal. I'm sure of it. We just want to see what it is."

He joined us, and we walked over to the bush. We pulled up the branches, and there lay Matt's bike. It wasn't damaged at all, so it didn't look like he'd crashed into the ravine.

"Over here!" my dad called to the others, who started running. "We've found Matt's bike!"

A ragged scrap of paper was impaled on the brake handle. "What's this?" Kamau asked, pulling it off the bike and opening it. I read it over his shoulder, but couldn't believe my eyes. I grabbed it from Kamau and gave it to my dad.

"It can't be true, Dad. It looks like a ransom note, but Matt can't have been kidnapped. That just can't have happened. We should never have given him number thirteen." I had to stop talking as I began to sob.

My dad read the note to the others: I have the boy. If you want to see him again, leave 10,000 shillings in this very spot.

Dad put his arm around Mr. Chadwick. "It looks bad," Dad said, "but we know the Lord is in control." Mr. Chadwick nodded, but I could see tears leaking from the edges of his eyes.

We had to tell the police, but we didn't want to lose the trail while it was still hot. My dad said, "I'm going back to Rugendo with the kids. I'll call the police and get more help."

"Please, Dad, can't you let Dave, Jon, Kamau, and me stay and help with the search," I begged. Reluctantly he agreed, but made us promise to stay close to Matt's dad. We promised.

"Can we girls stay, too, Mr. Sandler?" Jill asked.

My dad hesitated. Then he said, "I'm sure you'd be fine if you stayed and helped with the search, but I'm worried about what your parents might say. After all, there is a kidnapper loose here in the woods. I think you girls had better come with me."

"So why are you letting Dean and the Rhinos stay and not us," Jill demanded. "We can search as well as the boys."

"I'm sure you can," my dad said, "but I'd rather let your parents decide that. For now, it's best if you come with me."

Jill's face showed she wanted to argue some more. Instead she said, "We Cheetahs will discover what's happened to Matt."

We searched through lunch and well into the afternoon, without even stopping to eat. We found nothing. At about 4:00, my dad arrived with the Kenyan police and Dr. Freedman and Mr. Krenden. We searched until dark, but try as we might, we found no sign of Matt or his kidnapper.

It was as if the kidnapper had allowed us to find Matt's bike and then vanished, taking Matt with him.

We went home discouraged and very tired. What had begun as an exciting day for a bike race had ended in a nightmare.

That evening after supper everyone on the mission station gathered together, and we prayed long and hard for Matt's safe return. We contacted the mission office in Nairobi to have them pray. At the evening radio call, Mr. Krenden informed the other mission stations, and they all promised to pray as well.

When we left the prayer meeting, I knew we would find Matt. I didn't know how. Things looked hopeless, but while we had prayed

I'd been encouraged by the reminders of how great and strong God was and how he'd answered so many prayers before. I just wished there was something we could do.

Jill sidled up to me outside the meeting hall. "We Cheetahs have come up with a plan to rescue Matt," she said.

"What kind of a plan?" I asked. "How can you rescue Matt when you don't even know where he is?"

"You'll see," Jill answered mysteriously.

The next day a special unit of Kenyan policemen arrived with sniffing dogs, which yelped up a storm and crashed through a lot of bushes. But by the end of the day they hadn't uncovered anything new.

The police officer in charge asked some of the missionaries if they would pay the ransom money, since they had no idea what else to do. Matt's dad wanted to, of course, but the mission had a policy against paying ransoms, saying it could lead to more kidnappings in the future.

Finally the police left with their apologies for not solving the case. They promised to leave some plainclothes policemen working on it, but they called off the search parties. Whoever had snatched Matt had disappeared without a clue.

Dave, Jon, Kamau, and I had hung around with the missionary men and the police dogs all day. I felt my calf muscles twitching from all the walking we'd done. We hadn't seen the Cheetahs, and I wondered what they had been doing to find Matt.

"Come on," I called to the other boys. "Tomorrow morning we'll meet early and go to the clubhouse. We have to figure out some way to help Matt."

"What else can we do?" Jon asked, head sagging.

"We can ask God to help us come up with a plan," I said.

"Let's pray now," Kamau suggested.

I nodded. "Go ahead and pray, Kamau." We bowed our heads as Kamau prayed.

"Lord, we don't know what to do. We ask you to help us find a way to rescue Matt. We know you are powerful. Thank you for always hearing our prayers. Amen."

I looked at the others. With Matt gone, I'd started acting as the Rhinos' leader. "The Cheetahs said they had a plan to rescue Matt last night. I haven't seen them all day. I'm not sure how they plan to rescue him without knowing where he is, but Matt is our club captain. We're the ones who should save him."

CHAPTER EIGHT

THE MAU MAU CAVE

Hiking through the forest to our tree house in the early morning had a calming effect. Once in the clubhouse, I called our meeting to order.

"We need to decide what we can do to help Matt. The police have given up. Our parents don't seem to know what to do either. We're Matt's closest friends. It's up to us to do something." We sat silently, trying to think.

"I know," Jon said. "We could get a hot-air balloon and then go over the whole area looking down until we find him! It would be kind of like those deluxe safaris they arrange for tourists to see animals out on the Maasai Mara."

We thought about that suggestion. Dave, practical as usual, finally said, "It's a good idea, Jon, but I'm not sure it will work. First, we don't have a hot-air balloon. And second, whoever kidnapped Matt would have him hidden somewhere, and he'd probably be even harder to spot from the air. What we need to do is think of a place someone might use as a hiding place."

"The old Mau Mau cave!" Kamau said. "It's hidden away down in that ravine below Rugendo. It would be a perfect hideout."

"Good idea!" agreed Jon, already halfway down the ladder. Dave, Kamau, and I hurried to catch up. We loped through the forest in our unique Rhino half-jog that Matt had invented. Matt had explained that it helped us go the fastest while using the least amount of energy. Nobody had bothered to check if his theory was actually correct, and since he was our leader, that's how we moved through the forest.

The Mau Mau cave was a natural fault in a steep ravine fairly close to Rugendo. Trees and overhanging bushes choked the ravine, making it a dark and gloomy place. My dad told me it was unlikely the Mau Mau had ever used the cave as a hideout during Kenya's struggle for independence. However, ever since we'd known about the cave, we'd called it the Mau Mau cave.

After working our way through the bush for half an hour, we came to a six-foot cliff just above the cave. "Skss!" I hissed at Jon, using the African way of getting someone's attention. He stopped. "We have to plan how we'll do this," I whispered. "We can't just run in. If the kidnappers are there, they'll see us and escape."

Dave took off his glasses and wiped them on his Safari Rally T-shirt. He squinted and said, "I'll go above the cave and come down near the far side of the entrance. Jon, you wait here by this side of the cave. Dean, you and Kamau move into the bushes in front of the cave. Jon and I will enter the cave from opposite sides, and if we flush anyone out you two will have to stop them."

I felt my knees tremble at the thought of a kidnapper running at me. Maybe I'd act like I did in my first rugby scrimmage and fall on my face and let the kidnapper run right over me. I inwardly asked God to give me strength. At least I had Kamau next to me.

My heart thudded like a Kenyan church drum as we began to

carry out our plan. Kamau and I crawled on our bellies, hooking our elbows into the rotting leaf-mulch and pulling ourselves through the reedy grass. In front of the cave entrance, we hunched down behind a bushy green tree ready to explode out and tackle anyone who might try to escape. Jon and Dave arrived at opposite sides of the cave entrance, signaled to each other, and began to enter.

Jon and Dave hesitated for a moment. They were probably allowing their eyes to adjust to the gloom before they slipped silently in. Within seconds I couldn't see them. Only their footprints in the soft dust remained.

I crouched, ready. Suddenly something leaped on me from behind, knocking me flat on my face. "Help!" I shouted, "I'm being attacked."

I could hear Jon and Dave scrambling out of the cave as Kamau pulled someone off my back. I twisted around to look up at my attacker. "Freddie!" I shouted. "What are you doing jumping on me?"

Jill stepped out from behind a tree and called out, "False alarm, Cheetahs."

Standing up and dusting myself off, I demanded, "What's going on?" Dave and Jon had arrived by then, puzzled expressions on their faces.

Jill looked us over and said, "I should ask you the same question. We've set up a trap for the kidnappers, and you stumbled into it."

"Wait a minute," I said. "Just explain what you're up to."

The other Cheetahs appeared, and we sat down and listened as Jill explained how the Cheetahs had thought the kidnappers might use the Mau Mau cave as a hideout.

"We thought the same thing," Kamau said.

"But we thought of it first," Jill said. "We came yesterday and looked around. We saw some mysterious footprints, but no sign of Matt. We decided to come back today in case anyone showed up. We didn't want to be seen, so we stayed quite far back. When we heard a loud 'Skss!' we thought sure the kidnappers had come. Freddie jumped on the first kidnapper she saw, and we rushed out to join her."

"But I'm not a kidnapper," I said.

"We know that now," said Rachel. "But we only saw bushes moving, and someone hiding. Anyway, it looks like our idea didn't work. We only caught a few clumsy Rhinos."

"You didn't catch us," I pointed out. "You just surprised us."

"Maybe we can do a better job of finding Matt if we work together," I suggested. Dave and Jon both raised their eyebrows at the thought, but Dave shrugged and said, "Why not?"

Jon asked, "Where are those mysterious footprints? They may give us a clue of where to search next."

Jill nodded and led the way back toward the entrance of the cave. She knelt in the gray dust, which was as powdery as wheat flour. "Sorry," she announced, "it looks like your running around in here has covered up any footprints we saw yesterday."

Jon lifted his right hand and cocked his ear toward the cave. "I think I hear something," he hissed. He listened again, then stood up and called out, "We hear you! Come out of there and bring our friend Matt with you."

I crouched, ready to take action. Nothing happened. Jon, Dave, and Freddie edged closer and moved into the darkness of the cave. Suddenly Dave shouted, "Someone's throwing things at me!"

"Me too!" Freddie cried out. A few seconds later, all three tumbled out of the cave into the dust.

"Watch out!" yelled Jon. "He's coming! Be ready to grab him!"

Kamau and I ran forward only to be met by a whirling cloud of bats. They divided around us, using their sonar to see exactly where we stood. They whirred the air around our heads, but they didn't hit us.

"Bats!" I said, sitting down in the dust and laughing. "Is that all you found in there? Bats?"

Jon looked up sheepishly at the small black bats, which slowly circled back into the cave. "I thought someone was in there," he said. "I really did, but I guess it was just the bats squeaking. I should have known, but I was so sure we'd find Matt and the kidnapper here."

"Me too," said Dave, grinning, "And when that first bat made a pass by my ear, I thought someone was throwing rocks or shooting poisoned arrows. I just started to run."

"So did I," Freddie giggled.

"Bats!" I said as we began slapping the dust off our clothes. "Well, at least we can cross this cave off the list of places to search. I think we Rhinos will go back to our clubhouse to work on a better plan."

Kamau tapped me on the shoulder. "Someone's watching us," he said quietly. He pointed with his chin at a purple-flowered Cape chestnut tree. The brim of a ragged hat peeked out from behind it.

"What's up?" Jill asked. "What are you staring at?"

I thought I would have a heart attack as a powerfully-built Kenyan man stepped out of hiding and frowned at us. He wore a tattered green bush hat much like mine, but his hat rattled with the weight of about seven army combat medals and regalia from various army regiments. The man's muddy-brown eyes pierced through me. The whites were laced with red veins as fine as hairs. A front tooth was missing.

He stepped toward us, and the acrid scent of sweat and wood smoke from his ragged clothes made it hard to breathe. Sticks had tangled in the uncombed hair that crept out from under his hat. My feet felt like blocks of cement, and I couldn't run.

The man extended his left hand for me to shake. I wondered why he was using his left hand, but slowly stretched my left hand out toward him. Our hands met, and the older man smiled.

"Scout's handshake," he informed me, then greeted all of us before drawing himself tall and saluting. "Mwago Scout," he announced. "What for you come my forest?"

Kamau cowered behind me. "I've heard of Mwago," he whispered in my ear. "He's a crazy man who betrayed our Kikuyu people when he fought with the British against the Mau Mau. My people say his wife poisoned him. Since then, he's lived alone in the forest and thinks all Kikuyu are his enemies. He might hurt me."

I shiverered. Mwago looked crazy, but he didn't seem to be angry. "Uh," I began, "we're looking for our friend. He was kidnapped from Rugendo."

Mwago came closer. The sharp smoky smell of his ragged clothes clogged my nostrils. He grabbed Kamau by the shoulder. "My English no for the good. You boy, tell me, what for you come?"

Kamau's voice croaked in fear, but he told Mwago in Kikuyu what had happened to Matt.

"Me no for the see your friend," Mwago said after listening to

Kamau's explanation. We stood around Mwago, who sat on the grass and rubbed the gray stubble on his chin. I looked at Jill, and she shrugged.

Suddenly Mwago stood up. "Mau Mau, no for the good," he snorted, the anger evident in the way he spit the words out. He turned and spoke rapidly to Kamau, saluted all of us and marched into the forest, the medals clanking from his hat.

We all looked at Kamau. "He says Matt was kidnapped by Mau Mau freedom fighters. He said he would find them and rescue our friend."

"Do you think he really will?" Dave asked.

"I think he's crazy," Kamau said. "I'm not sure he even knows what he'll do next. My parents say he wanders through the forest, sleeping under trees or making small shelters. When someone sees him, he thinks they are the Mau Mau—his enemies. Afraid that they'll know where he's staying, he moves and builds another hide-out." Kamau took a deep breath. "This is the first time I've met Mwago. I doubt he'll rescue Matt for us. I'm just glad he didn't hurt us."

"Well, Matt sure isn't here at the cave," concluded Jill. "Come on girls. Let's go to my house to think about what to do next." Turning to me, she went on, "Maybe we can meet this afternoon and compare plans."

I nodded. "We'll see." I wondered what Matt would think if the Cheetahs claimed credit for finding and rescuing him. But at this point, I just wanted him home and safe and would even give up our Rhino pride to see it happen.

SETTING THE TRAP

We headed back to our tree house. I felt as thirsty as a camel after forty days in the desert. "Let's drink *chai* while we think," I said, and Dave, Jon, and Kamau agreed. I climbed up the tree and tossed some matches down to Jon. Dave was already collecting firewood. I gathered some tea leaves in a small yellow packet with smudged green lettering, an old black-bottomed tin pot, a plastic tea strainer, some dried milk, sugar, and four battered enamel mugs and climbed back down.

While Jon and Dave got the fire going, Kamau filled the pot with water from a nearby stream. He fished out the small black tadpoles with the tea-stained plastic tea strainer and tossed them back into the stream.

We shook the tea leaves, dried milk, and sugar into the water and boiled the mixture, stirring it occasionally with a stick that Jon cut from a wild olive tree.

When the *chai* was ready, we poured it into our mugs and drank it with noisy sucking noises. We'd all learned how to do this on visits to Kikuyu homes near Rugendo. It was a good way to keep your tongue from getting burned, since sucking over the hot tea before it entered your mouth cooled off the boiling-hot drink.

Suddenly the bushes parted and Mwago appeared. He squatted next to the fire and lifted up the pot. The remaining caramel-colored *chai* swished around the bottom. Mwago put the pot to his lips and slurped down a large mouthful. He smiled and licked his lips. We sat like statues, not sure how to react.

I felt something burn my hand and looked down to see my mug of *chai* spilling over the sides as I trembled. I set the mug on the grass.

Mwago stood up. He stared at me and then stalked slowly toward me. I stopped breathing. He reached down and stroked my bush hat. I thought maybe he wanted to trade, so I took my hat off. Mwago had a faraway look in his eyes. His bloodshot eyes squinted as he continued to stare at me. He shook his head then saluted again. This time, he aimed his salute at me alone.

"*Asante kwa chai*, thanks for the tea. Me find Mau Mau," Mwago said. "Me find your friend." He slipped away through the trees.

I used the back of my hand to wipe away the sweat that had beaded on my forehead. "He's a weird guy," I said.

Kamau could only nod.

"He scares me," Dave said.

We finished our fast cooling mugs of *chai* and put out the fire, then climbed back up the tree house for more privacy as we talked.

I had an idea. "Listen," I said. "The last real clue we have about Matt's kidnapping is the bush where his bike was hidden with the ransom note, right?"

"Right," said Dave.

"Well," I said slowly, "instead of trying to find Matt out there somewhere, why don't we go back to that spot. The kidnapper did ask for a ransom. Maybe he'll come back to that bush looking for the ransom money. He doesn't know our parents agreed not to leave any money. If we go there and wait, maybe the kidnapper will come and we can catch him."

Jon said excitedly, "We can do even better than that. We can put some money in an envelope. When the kidnapper comes, he'll be distracted while he checks out how much money is there, and we can run out of our hiding place and tie him up."

"Good idea," I said. "How much money do we have, Dave?" He fished a key from his pocket and opened our treasury. We only had a soft, wrinkled fifty-shilling note left in the old box we used to hide our money. "It'll have to do," I said. "After all, we're not really paying a ransom, just trying to bait a trap."

Dave frowned. "But with only one measly fifty-shilling note in the envelope, the kidnapper will be able to feel immediately there's not enough money. We need him to be counting something so we can jump him."

"You're right," I said, scratching my chin.

"Maybe the Cheetahs can help," Kamau said.

"Good idea, Kamau," I said. "The Cheetahs wanted to meet this afternoon to compare plans. We can ask them for more money."

Dave nodded. He wrapped the fifty shillings in an old envelope and wrote RANSOM MONEY in big letters, but didn't seal the envelope. We climbed down the tree and did the Rhino half-jog back to Rugendo. We agreed to meet after lunch and go to Jill's before taking the envelope to the bush where Matt's bike had been found.

"Your idea might work," Jill said when I explained our plan.

She called Rebekah, Rachel, and Freddie and told them to bring some cash.

Rachel was reluctant to part with her hundred shilling note. "Are you sure this will work?" she asked. Jon explained again how we'd use the envelope to trap the kidnapper.

"What if he doesn't come?" Rebekah asked.

"Then we take the envelope and go home," said Dave.

"And give us our money back?" Freddie asked.

"Yes, of course we'll give everyone their money back." Dave was clearly annoyed. "Now can we get on with our plan? If we take too long, the afternoon will be gone."

"I guess our money will be safe," Rachel said. "But I think we should join you in setting up the trap. Don't you, Jill?"

"Absolutely," Jill answered.

"But—" Jon started to protest.

"We'll all go together," I cut Jon off. "It will give us a better chance of catching the kidnapper."

Between the four Cheetahs they had three hundred shillings; two fifty-shilling notes and two one-hundred shilling notes. So Dave added their money to our fifty shillings and wadded the notes up to make it seem thicker than it really was and shoved it into the ransom envelope. We hiked to the bush where Matt's bike had been found.

When we arrived, Jon looked around and found some low trees thick with leaves. "We'll have a perfect lookout if we hide up there," he said. Freddie clambered up the first tree even before we put the money under the bush. Jill tied a red strip of cloth to the bush to attract the kidnapper's attention. We all climbed the trees to join Freddie.

Kamau and I shared a branch. I jammed my foot in a crotch to balance myself, then wedged my back against the tree trunk. We waited and waited. After an hour, I whispered to the others, "I'm thirsty; did anyone bring anything to drink?" No one had. So we all waited, hot and thirsty. Nothing happened. My leg muscles started to cramp. "I need to move," I said into Kamau's ear and pushed with my left foot, trying to find another, more comfortable position, but in doing so, I broke a small branch. It snapped with a loud crack.

Jon looked at me angrily and hissed, "If anyone wanted to come and check for the ransom, he'd have left by now with all the noise you're making." We were all irritable. Hiking is fun. Waiting is agony, especially when you're balanced on a branch in a tree.

It was now about 4:30 P.M. "Let's give it up," I said. Jill nodded in agreement as she struggled to free a tress of hair tangled in a tree branch.

"It was a good idea," she said, "but I guess it didn't work." Kamau and I started to clamber down from the tree. Suddenly Jon waved frantically and pointed.

We looked and saw someone crouched behind a rock near the bush where we'd left the envelope of money. It looked like a young Kenyan boy, and I doubted he would be the kidnapper, but maybe he'd been sent as a messenger. The boy darted to the bush, seized the envelope, and began to run away without counting it.

"That's Mburu!" Kamau said to me. "I attend school with him."

"After him!" I shouted as I slid the rest of the way down the tree. Jill, Rachel, and Rebekah outran all of us Rhinos, but the Kenyan boy must have been related to one of the Kenyan runners who ran in the Olympics. He left us behind, but we could see he was running straight for Rugendo. Though we couldn't keep up with him, we could watch his progress as we left the forest. He ran through some cornfields, but the green corn plants stood only a few feet high so we could see where he went.

He arrived at a small wooden house near the Rugendo Hospital and went in. We stopped and looked at each other. "The house belongs to Mburu's father who works in the hospital as a lab technician," Kamau informed us.

"Could Mburu's father know what had happened to Matt?" asked Jill. "Did he help arrange the kidnapping?"

"Our plan worked, you guys," I said, excitedly. "This is a real clue, the first since we found Matt's bike and the ransom note. We haven't caught the kidnapper yet, but Mburu and his dad must be a link. Jon and Dave, you stay and watch the house. Kamau and I will get our parents and tell them what we've found out."

"Stay with Dave and Jon," Jill instructed Rachel and Rebekah. "Freddie and I will go with Dean and Kamau."

As we ran to my house, Kamau said, "I don't understand how Mburu and his father could be mixed up in Matt's kidnapping. Mburu's parents attend a mid-week church prayer fellowship at our home. And Mburu never misses learning his Bible verse for Sunday school. "

"It doesn't make sense," I agreed. "But we have to check it out."

At home I explained everything to my dad. He called Matt's dad, and we all hurried to the house by the hospital.

When we got there, Jon and Dave stepped out from behind a tree. "No one has left the house. So we know Mburu's still in there," Jon said.

Rachel and Rebekah joined us from where they'd been watching the back door. "We're sure this boy will lead us to Matt's kidnapper," Rachel said.

Matt's dad knocked on the door and the lab technician came out and greeted us warmly. "*Karibu*, welcome," he said, ushering us into the sitting room. We all squeezed onto a set of gold-colored couches and chairs covered with white hand-knitted doilies. The lab technician offered us *chai*. Matt's dad thanked him, but said we'd come about some urgent business. He told him what we had seen.

The man's eyes narrowed, and he called loudly, "Mburu, please come out here." The young boy we had chased came slowly into the room, eyes staring at the floor.

Kamau averted his eyes and wouldn't look at Mburu.

"That's him," Jon accused. "He went to the bush where we found Matt's bike and collected an envelope of money we had placed there hoping to lure the kidnapper. He must know something about it. He must be a messenger for the kidnapper."

The lab technician questioned his son, "Did you take an envelope with money in it?"

"Yes, father," Mburu answered.

"Go bring it to me," his father instructed.

Mburu went out and brought back the envelope with the 350 shillings still inside.

"How did you get tangled up with the kidnappers?" his father asked.

Mburu mumbled something.

"Speak louder," his father demanded.

"I heard about the ransom note. I thought if I waited, I might get some free money. I've been checking that bush every day since the missionary boy was kidnapped. Today I found this envelope and came here with it. But I know nothing about the kidnappers."

Mburu's father scolded him for being greedy. He turned to Matt's father. "I'm sorry. We are all very worried about your son." He handed back the envelope with the money.

Our dads thanked him and apologized for scaring Mburu. We all prayed together for Matt's safe recovery. As we prayed, Kamau sidled up to Mburu and put his arm around his school friend.

After the others had gone home, I said to my dad, "Well, we tried, but I guess our plan wasn't so hot."

He put his hand on my shoulder and consoled me. "It was a good plan. I'm just sorry it didn't work out. We're all worried about Matt. And it's good to see you boys trying your best to help your friend. We'll find Matt. I'm sure of it."

CHAPTER TEN

REVEREND KIMANI

The next day Dave, Jon, Kamau, and I had no more ideas on how to help Matt. Our first two plans hadn't been exactly successful. So we decided to work off our frustration by riding bikes. It had poured the night before, and the road had melted into a muddy sauce the color of burned gravy. We skidded around corners and splashed through the puddles that were scattered on the road like haphazardly thrown rugs.

By midmorning it was time for a break. We rode our bikes across Rugendo to the *dukas,* as we called the row of one-room stores that sold everything from cornmeal and sugar to brightly colored balls of bubble gum and Eveready batteries. We pulled up outside the *chai* house and squinted in the gloom as we stepped inside.

"*Chai* and a *mandazi,*" we told the waiter as we sat at a wobbly table with legs all cut to different lengths. *Mandazis* are a kind of square doughnut without a hole.

The young man in the green, flour-stained apron returned with the *chai.* The *mandazi* came a few minutes later wrapped in old newspaper that oozed oil onto the plate. An old man in the corner poured his *chai* out of his cup onto the saucer before drinking it.

We tried it, too. It did an even better job of cooling down the tea than loud sucking. We ripped pieces off our *mandazi* and dunked them into our *chai* before eating them.

The table wobbled again, and Dave spilled some of his *chai*. "I know how to fix it," Kamau said. He ripped a piece of the oily newspaper and folded it carefully into a wad about half-an-inch thick. He leaned down and wedged the paper under the shortest table leg. It helped, but the table still seesawed every time one of us put an elbow on it.

I had a piece of *mandazi* soaking in my *chai* when I heard some-one outside say in a loud voice, "*Wi mwega,* are you well, Bwana Kimani?" Now, Kimani is a common name, but on this day the name jolted my memory. Reverend Kimani who had spoken in church—the one I thought we'd seen at the oathing ceremony! The one who had stared right at Matt! And, come to think of it, maybe even the same face I'd seen in the forest when we were setting up the bike safari route on the old slave trail.

"Ouch!" I cried out. I dropped my *mandazi* in the tea and pulled my hand out of my *chai* mug.

"Hey, Dean, are you OK?" asked Dave.

"Yes," I answered, sucking my burned fingers. "I just need to check something." I stepped outside to see which Kimani had been passing. A man in a suit coat entered the *duka* next to the *chai* house.

I followed him in and slid along the dirty glass counter to the corner. It was the same Reverend Kimani! His right pants leg was tucked into his sock as though to keep it from tangling in a bike chain. He was buying several loaves of bread, as well as jam, sugar, flour, and some biscuits, as cookies are called in Kenya.

"You've come a long way," the shopkeeper said to Reverend Kimani. "There are many stores closer to your home than my little shop. And why are you buying white man's food? Are you expecting some guests?"

"Yes, yes, I know there are shops closer to my house," Reverend Kimani said. He seemed irritated by the shopkeeper's comments about his purchases. "I came to visit my cousin who is the pastor here in Rugendo. I decided to buy some things here since we are expecting some missionaries to visit us soon."

I tried to slink deeper into the darkness of the corner. Reverend Kimani had told a lie. Pastor Kariuki, his cousin, was away for a one-week evangelism campaign at the coast. I didn't know if Reverend Kimani really had any missionaries who were going to visit, but I had a pretty good idea who he might be buying the bread and jam for.

Just then the shopkeeper's son came over to where I stood. I didn't want Reverend Kimani to notice me. "Some Black Cat," I said as quietly as I could, pointing at the licorice gum in a plastic jar with a blue screw-on lid.

"How many?" the young man asked. By now I was sure Reverend Kimani would see me and recognize me, but he was fumbling in his pocket and counting out change. I pulled out two shillings and croaked, "Two please." I snatched the gum he pushed across the scarred glass counter, slipped out the door, and ran to the *chai* house.

"Hey, Dean, we were getting ready to drink your *chai,* but there's a piece of soggy *mandazi* floating in it," Jon teased. Then he saw my face. "What is it, Dean? You look like you've seen a leopard's tail dangling from a tree."

"I think I've found Matt's kidnapper," I said sitting down and gulping my *chai,* floating *mandazi* and all.

"How?" Jon questioned.

I leaned forward and whispered, "There isn't time to explain everything right now. But I'm pretty sure that the man who kidnapped Matt is in the *duka* next door buying supplies. His name is Reverend Kimani and we have to leave here quietly and follow him on our bikes without being noticed."

"Reverend Kimani?" Kamau asked. "He can't be the kidnapper. He's a pastor. Why would he kidnap Matt?"

"I know it sounds crazy, but I'm sure I'm right," I said. "Now, act normally and do what I say. I'll explain later."

Dave, Kamau, and Jon shrugged, but they did what I said. All we had to do was wait and watch until Reverend Kimani got on his big black bicycle, probably a Hero Jet like Kamau rode. It seemed like all Kenyan men in rural areas drove big black bicycles with iron carriers behind the seat for luggage or passengers. When he got on his bike, we would see which direction he took and then follow at a distance. It would be easy to follow the tracks his bike tires made in the soft Rugendo mud. Maybe God had sent the rain and mud in answer to our prayers.

My mind was still trying to work out exactly why Reverend Kimani would have kidnapped Matt. He may have thought Matt could identify him as a Christian who had bowed to pressure and taken the secret oath. Perhaps he thought Matt would tell his dad, and Reverend Kimani feared he would be kicked out of the pastorate. Somehow I knew Matt's kidnapping tied in with the secret oathing ceremony we'd seen.

Just then Reverend Kimani passed by the *chai* house carrying his purchases in a woven sisal basket. I let a few seconds pass before I leaned forward and hissed, "Outside, now! And be as inconspicuous as possible."

Jon, Dave, and Kamau shook their heads at what they thought was my outrageous behavior, but we all went out. Reverend Kimani was just getting onto his bicycle. He rode off down the dirt road that eventually led to Nairobi. There were a lot of places to turn off before Nairobi, so I knew we'd have to watch closely.

"We can't lose that man," I said. "But we can't let him know we're following him either. Kamau, maybe you should go first. He might get nervous if he sees three white boys riding after him."

"What should I do?" Kamau asked, mounting his bike.

"Just follow until he turns off somewhere. We won't be far behind," I said.

Kamau nodded and pushed off, his tires squishing in the mud.

"I'm not sure about this," Jon said, looking dubious. "Why do you think this pastor is Matt's kidnapper?"

"Because," I said, pausing for emphasis, "I'm convinced he's the man we saw at the oathing ceremony." Dave had bought some extra *mandazis* and put them in a plastic bag. I hastily tied the bag to my handlebars as I went on, "I'm sure he's the one who kidnapped Matt, but we have to follow him to prove anything. I saw him buy bread and jam, and I'm positive it's for Matt to eat. We have to find out where he's hiding Matt so we can rescue him."

Just then Jill and the Cheetahs rode up, their legs freckled with mud spatters. "What are you guys up to?" Freddie blurted out.

"Quiet!" I hissed, still gazing at Reverend Kimani as he rode away. The girls looked shocked at my strong rebuke. Reverend Kimani turned on his bike to look back. Kamau skidded to a stop and got off his bike. I wondered what Reverend Kimani thought about a Kenyan boy riding behind and seven missionary kids astride bikes on the muddy lane next to the *dukas*. Reverend Kimani's bike swerved as he regained his balance from his backward glance. He rounded the corner where the lone yellow fever tree stood.

"Follow him!" I said to Jon and Dave. I looked at Jill. "I think we've found Matt's kidnapper." I'd already pushed off. "We can't have too many people following him or he'll see us for sure. Go tell our parents we're hot on Matt's trail. Tell them to be ready. We'll send a message as soon as we're sure where Matt is being hidden."

A puzzled look crossed Jill's face as she absorbed my words. "But where? Can't we come?" she called. I waved and pedaled hard to catch up with the others. The plastic bag of *mandazis* on my handlebars flapped in the wind as I picked up speed.

We rode up to the yellow fever tree and watched Kamau's back vanishing slowly around the next bend. There was a long mud puddle in the road. Reverend Kimani's and Kamau's bicycles had made tracks in the soft mud around the edges.

Jon jumped down and squatted by the tire tracks. "Kamau's bike has new tires, so these are his tracks," he said after a few seconds. I could easily make out the studded pattern. "Reverend Kimani's tires are more worn. And look at this. He must have had a bad puncture once. There's a regular square mark here that doesn't match the tire pattern. That happens sometimes with a patch. With a mark like that it will be easy to identify his tracks."

Dave and I nodded wisely. I was glad Jon had the ability to notice things. I sure wouldn't have thought to look closely at the tire tracks. Nor would I have picked out what Jon had seen. But now that we knew, we hoped the information would be useful.

We followed Kamau, catching glimpses of him as we came to corners. We kept well back so that even if Reverend Kimani turned around, he'd only see Kamau.

I signaled for the other two to stop. "We're coming up to Makutano village," I said. "We need to decide what to do before we get there." Makutano meant "meeting place" and although it started with only a few *dukas,* it had grown to a sizable village with two big market days each week. "First, we need to catch up with Kamau. When we can see the village from that hill over there, we'll all wait and watch. If Reverend Kimani passes through the village and keeps going, we'll see which road he goes on. Then we can follow."

"But if he stops in the village, we'll lose sight of him," Dave pointed out.

"Yeah, but then we can go down and try to follow his tracks in town," Jon said. "With that square patch on Reverend Kimani's tire and last night's rain, we should be able track him. I'm glad it's muddy. It would be almost impossible to follow anyone's bike tracks during the dry season when the road is hard as iron."

We set off again, overtaking Kamau. "Good work, Kamau," I said as we pulled up at the hill overlooking Makutano.

Kamau panted as he said, "I'm glad we're together again. " Looking down, we saw Reverend Kimani getting close to the village. Once in the village, we lost sight of him. We waited, watching in case he would reappear on one of the other roads leading from the village, but we saw nothing. He must have entered a building.

"We'll have to track him," Jon said.

Just then I heard a soft hissing sound, almost like a puff adder.

CHAPTER ELEVEN

REPAIRING A FLAT TIRE

I reached back and pinched my rear tire. It was soft and getting softer. "Oh, no!" I said. "I have a puncture. Did any of you bring a repair kit?"

Dave, Kamau, and Jon shook their heads. "We weren't expecting a long bike ride this morning when we went to the *chai* house," Dave said.

Suddenly I remembered the Black Cat gum I'd bought earlier while eavesdropping on Reverend Kimani. Pulling the gum out of my pocket, I said, "I can repair my tire with this gum, at least for a while. But it will take a bit of time without tools. You guys had better go into Makutano and trace Reverend Kimani. I'll catch up either by following his tracks or else one of you can wait for me at the crossroads in town."

Kamau, Jon, and Dave agreed and rode down the hill into the village. I popped the gum into my mouth and started chewing so it would be ready to seal the puncture. It was almost eleven in the morning, and the burning sun made sweat drip off my forehead like rain off a corrugated iron roof. I took off my bush hat and wiped my head before pulling my bike off the road and pushing it under the shade of a large cabbage tree.

I struggled to get my wheel off without tools. I had to bang the nuts with a rock until they were loose enough to undo by hand. It scraped the skin off my knuckles, but at least I had the wheel off.

I needed something to stretch the tire off the rim so I tried using a stick, but the stick kept breaking. I hunted around until I found a sharp piece of obsidian rock, or black volcanic glass, the debris from a volcanic eruption some centuries before. The rock was sharp on one side but thick on the other. The thick end fit nicely into my hand. I wondered if it might be a prehistoric hand axe like the ones Louis Leakey and other scientists had found around Kenya. I made note of the place in case we ever wanted to come back and do some digging for hand axes. Using the rock, I managed to force the sharp edge between the tire and the rim, and soon I had the tire free and the tube out.

In the tube I found the problem. A small thorn had made a hole. I removed the thorn and applied the licorice chewing gum to the hole. I really plastered the gum on. It needed to hold until I got home. I ran my finger around inside the tire to be sure there were no more thorns or small rocks to cause another puncture.

I had remounted the tire and started to use the hand pump I always carried on the frame of my bike when I heard voices on the road.

"*Wi mwega,* are you well, Bwana Kimani?" a voice said.

Kimani? I wondered if it was our Reverend Kimani. I looked carefully. It was! What had happened to Kamau, Dave, and Jon? I didn't know, but I dropped to my stomach and crawled behind a bush to listen.

After sitting through so many Kikuyu church services, I understood a bit of the language. I couldn't speak it much, but I could usually understand what people were saying. Reverend Kimani explained to his friend how he had just returned a bike to his brother in Makutano. "Bike" is an easy word to pick out. It has been adapted from the English—*baisikeli*.

"I used the *baisikeli* to go to Rugendo on business," Reverend Kimani said, "and now that I've returned it, I'm going to my garden to check on how the maize is doing." Reverend Kimani carried the black plastic bag with the food he'd bought at the *duka*. The two men shook hands and parted.

I watched Reverend Kimani walk about twenty-five yards before turning down a narrow path. Since he still had his bag of food, I figured he hadn't yet gone to where Matt was hidden. It was up to me to follow him. Dave, Kamau, and Jon would still be looking for nonexistent bike tracks leading out of Makutano while the bike was parked in Reverend Kimani's brother's house.

I pumped my tire as fast as I could, but I was in too much of a hurry trying to get the wheel back on, and I pinched my index finger between the chain and the sprocket. I jumped back with pain and sucked my finger. When I took my finger out, there were two nasty blood blisters in the shape of the sprockets.

But I had to follow Reverend Kimani! I couldn't lose him when we seemed so close to finding Matt! Ignoring the ache in my finger, I went back to work and finally got the wheel back on. It wobbled when I rode it because I could only hand-tighten the nuts, but wobbly or not, riding my bike was faster than walking. I came to the path where Reverend Kimani had turned. Suddenly I realized I had to leave some sort of message for Dave, Kamau, and Jon or they wouldn't know where I'd gone.

I dismounted and dropped my bike on its side. I gathered stones and piled them together in what I hoped looked like an arrow pointing toward the path. *It's not the greatest arrow*, I thought, *but it should catch their attention*. I took a stick and scratched out a message in the mud. It read, "Matt's this way. Please hurry. Dean."

Satisfied with my message, I jumped onto my bike and rode down the path.

The path narrowed and branches clutched at my shoulders from both sides. It descended through the thick forest into one of the many ravines that scarred the hills in that area. As the path grew steeper, I began to go faster and faster. I gripped my brakes, but nothing happened. Because of my fear of hills and constantly grabbing my brake handles, I had worn the brakes so thin they couldn't stop me now.

I careened down the path, and the only thing I could think of to stop myself would be to crash into the bushes that choked the edges of the path. I didn't know which bushes might be filled with wickedly curved wait-a-bit thorns. Nor could I guess from the blur of green which patches hid the stinging nettles that infested these forests. So I gripped my brakes hard and tried not to close my eyes.

Suddenly I came around a corner and found myself approaching a narrow bridge over a small river at the bottom of the ravine. On the other side of the river, the path went up the slope. I'd made it. I could coast to a stop on the uphill side, but I faced a final hurdle. The bridge was made from six narrow poles lashed together and stretched over the river. The poles weren't entirely straight. Dark nasty cracks showed between them, but I was going too fast to stop.

I could head my bike off the four-foot path into the river, or try to lift the front wheel like a motorcycle stuntman and hope I reached the other side of the river. I decided to cross.

When my front wheel hit the bridge, it slipped off the round pole and plunged into a crack. My bike stopped very quickly. But I didn't. I flew over the handlebars and hit the edge of the bridge before bouncing and falling into the river. I found myself sitting in two feet of muddy water in the river.

I looked up and saw my bike wedged between two of the bridge poles. My handlebars were bent sideways. I guess I'd been reluctant to let go when my bike stopped. I found myself panting to catch my breath. Slowly, I stood up. My hip hurt. I seemed to remember hitting it on the side of the bridge. My wrist ached as well, and it had a red mark on it. Otherwise, I seemed to be OK.

Boy, I thought, *I hope the other guys have better brakes than I do.* Bending down, I picked up my bush hat from where it had landed in the river. I squeezed it, and muddy water dripped out. I put the still-wet hat on my head. The cool dampness felt good on my sweaty head.

After climbing up the riverbank, I reached for a handful of leaves, checking carefully to see that they weren't stinging nettles. I used the leaves to wipe the mud off and to dry myself as best I could. I walked onto the bridge, which was much easier to negotiate on foot. After tugging hard I freed my bike and wheeled it onto the far side of the river. I stood in front of it, gripped the front wheel between my knees and straightened them. They felt pretty loose. I knew I'd have to get out a wrench and tighten the bolt when I got home. But now I had to find out where Reverend Kimani had taken Matt. If he had taken Matt. I didn't even have any proof about that. Really, I was just guessing. *What if I'm wrong?* I thought. *Maybe I should go back and find Kamau, Jon, and Dave at Makutano.*

I stopped to ask God to help me find Matt and not to give up. I knew that even if I might be wrong, I had to keep trying. Taking my bike, I started pushing it along the path that angled steeply up the hill.

Just then a blue monkey gave its shrill nasal alarm cry. I realized Reverend Kimani was still ahead of me. He must have startled a troop of monkeys. They traveled in groups of ten to fifteen in these hills. I knew I had to keep following. But where were Kamau, Dave, and Jon? If they'd only catch up soon I wouldn't feel so alone.

Alone? I'd just prayed to the Lord and knew he was with me. My parents taught me that God was always there. But I still wished Dave, Kamau, and Jon would catch up—and soon! I gritted my teeth and pushed my bike up the path, which was blocked in places by big rocks and mud that had slid down the steep hillside after the recent rains.

Sweat trickled off my nose. The sun burned my fair freckled skin. The hill on this side of the ravine didn't have as many trees. I looked at the shadows and judged the time to be a little after noon. The sun felt like a hammer pounding down. The rocks radiated with the heat, but I kept pushing my bike up the hill. Finally I arrived at the top. Ahead of me was a plateau with fields of maize plants growing, young and green. Other fields had been planted in potatoes, and the dark green plants were full of lovely white flowers, evidence of the good rains.

I leaned my bike against a tree and scanned the horizon to find Reverend Kimani. This must have been an area recently opened up for farming because I could see only one or two small huts. They were shelters built to shield against the midday sun when the farmers came to dig on their land. The people lived in villages like Makutano on the other side of the ridge.

A man moved along the path toward one of the small huts. I marked it in my mind as about halfway between a wild olive tree and a large boulder. At this distance I couldn't tell for sure if it was Reverend Kimani, but since I could see no other sign of life, I assumed it must be. And what better place to hide Matt? Nervousness made my stomach all wiggly, as if flying ants were tickling my insides with their long, feathery wings.

I hoped Dave, Jon, and Kamau would catch up soon or that our parents would arrive with the Cheetahs. *But how can the Cheetahs come with our parents since they don't know where I am?* My heart sank. If they didn't come, I'd have to get closer by myself and see if Matt was OK. But it would be easier to sneak down to the hut later in the afternoon as it got dark.

Suddenly I felt hungry. I remembered the *mandazi* tied to my handlebars. The plastic bag had torn a bit from my wreck, but I unstrapped it and started to eat. Cold grease oozed out as I bit into the first *mandazi*, but when you're hungry, even a cold *mandazi* tastes good.

As I sat in the shade by my bike eating, something crashed in the trees behind me.

BLUE MONKEYS

The crashing noise startled me. Was Reverend Kimani rushing at me? Or was a Cape buffalo charging me through the brush? I had shinnied halfway up the nearest tree before I realized where the noise came from.

The trees swayed with the weight of a troop of blue monkeys. A few of them jumped from tree to tree, clutching at the ends of branches, hanging and kicking as they scrabbled for a better grip. Then, regaining their balance, they would leap again. Others leaned with their backs against the trunks of the trees and stared at me.

I felt foolish. *My imagination is running wild,* I thought. These must be the monkeys I had heard earlier screeching at Reverend Kimani. Reverend Kimani had probably thrown a rock or something at them to keep them from coming too close to the small farms on the plateau.

The monkeys settled down and looked at me. I began to lose my grip on the tree. My arm muscles were tired and a stinging pain told me I had scraped my knees. I slowly slid down the trunk.

Now that I was on the ground, the monkeys became uneasy again and began chattering. They sounded rather like birds chirping. I could see their silvery-white collars underlining their charcoal gray faces. I didn't want to scare them. If I did, they might scream with their loud EEE-yonk cry. That sound carried for miles, and Reverend Kimani would know someone else had disturbed the monkeys. If he did have Matt in the hut, he would be on the alert. He might even take Matt somewhere else.

Moving slowly so I wouldn't frighten the monkeys, I edged over to where I had dropped my half-eaten *mandazi* in my frantic scramble up the tree. I broke it into several small pieces. I didn't dare throw the pieces to the monkeys. They might think I was throwing rocks, and they'd make noise for sure. I slowly walked along, placing chunks of *mandazi* below the trees where the monkeys sat. My unhurried motions must have calmed them, because the chatter died down.

After laying out the pieces of *mandazi,* I returned to my bike and sat down. I looked down at the farms to see if I could catch a glimpse of Reverend Kimani or Matt. Without turning my head too far, I could still see the monkeys out of the corner of my eye.

For about ten minutes nothing happened. Then curiosity took over. A big monkey began to clamber slowly down from his perch. He hopped to the ground and cautiously crept up to the closest piece of *mandazi.* Sitting beside it, the monkey gingerly picked it up and examined it. He raised it to his nose and sniffed at it. Apparently he didn't like the smell of the oil it had been fried in because he wrinkled up his nose and dropped the *mandazi.* But after a few minutes he reached for it again. This time he nibbled at it. The taste must have been better than the smell because after the first nibble, he stuffed the whole thing into his mouth. This signaled the rest of the monkeys. Within seconds they had swooped down to the ground and eaten up all the *mandazi* chunks. They all looked at me and began edging closer. I guess they wanted more.

I showed them my empty hands in a gesture I hoped would tell them I didn't have anything else to give them. They didn't understand human body language and crept closer. Now what could I do? Climbing a tree sure wouldn't help me escape from monkeys. I knew monkeys didn't normally attack people, but I was alone and their fangs looked sharp.

I began to pray. Most of the time I forget to pray until I've tried everything else. Maybe that's the way most people are.

As the big male came within three feet, my heartbeat must have tripled. I saw the newspaper that the *mandazi* had been wrapped in before being put in the plastic bag. I crumpled up the newspaper and tossed it as far as I could. The monkeys all scrambled after the wadded up garbage, drawn by its shape and the oil that soaked it.

While the monkeys tussled over the newspaper and tore it to shreds, I jumped onto my bike and pedaled a safe distance away from the trees. About one hundred yards away I came to a big boulder. I turned my bike into the shade of the giant rock and got off and looked back. The monkeys were still squabbling over the newspaper. Blue monkeys don't like to go too far from trees, so I hoped I would be safe. After a few minutes they tired of the newspaper. They looked briefly in my direction, but then the big male climbed a tree. Branches swayed and crashed as the troop retreated into the forest.

I took a big breath in relief. "Thanks, God, for helping me to think of the newspaper," I prayed. "I'm scared, so please bring Kamau, Dave, and Jon to find me soon, and please, Lord, help us to find Matt." Feeling better, I slumped down and leaned my back against the coolness of the boulder. I closed my eyes for what seemed like minutes, but must have been quite awhile, because when I opened them again, the position of the sun told me it was late afternoon. Across the plateau, wisps of smoke rose from the hut where Reverend Kimani had entered earlier. That meant he had started a cooking fire. If Matt were in there, at least he wouldn't be starving to death.

I sat for a long time. Now it was getting late and the sun began to dip behind the volcanic mountain craters to the west. I started to devise a plan to rescue Matt by myself. Inwardly I trembled at the thought, but I had to do something. Matt was my best friend. I would wait another half hour. If no one came by then, I would sneak down to the hut on foot. If Matt was there I would rescue him, and we'd run to my bike and ride double back to the road—if my chewing gum-patched tire could handle the load.

And what about Reverend Kimani? What if he tried to stop me? I knew I couldn't overpower him. I thought and thought, but could find no answer to that problem. *Well,* I thought, *I'll just have to solve that problem later. Somehow.*

Just then I heard a rattling sound behind me. Instinctively, I ducked and hid from view. Within seconds a bike whizzed by. It was Jon. I jumped up. "Jon! Jon!" I called.

Jon whirled his head around and on seeing me his face broke into a grin. Braking to a stop, he came back. "Dean, am I ever glad to see you," he began.

I put my upright forefinger in front of my lips to tell him to talk quietly, and we sat down together behind the boulder. I told him how I'd followed Reverend Kimani and how I felt sure he had Matt held in a hut below us. I pointed it out to Jon.

"So tell me how you found me," I said.

Jon, Dave, and Kamau had followed Reverend Kimani's bike tracks into Makutano. "But we lost the tracks in the town. There was just too much traffic. We thought Reverend Kimani might be drinking tea someplace so we bought some sodas at a kiosk and waited. We searched every road leading out of Makutano, but we couldn't find his tire tracks anywhere."

"So what did you do next?" I asked.

"We were just about to give up and go back and pick you up so we could go home when Dave noticed a big, black bike leaning against a house. We decided to have a closer look."

"Reverend Kimani's bike," I interrupted. "He returned it to his brother. I found out when Reverend Kimani came by the path where I was fixing my bike."

"You're right," Jon nodded. "It turned out to be the bike Reverend Kimani had been riding. It had a big, square patch on the outside of the tire. Kamau asked a few questions, and we learned Reverend Kimani had gone to check on his maize *shamba*. The man who told us pointed with his chin in this direction and said the fields were on the other side of the ridge. So we rode back up the road to find you."

"Did you find my sign?" I asked.

Jon laughed. "It wasn't too hard. It looked like a roadblock, you used so many stones!"

"Sorry," I said. "I just didn't want you to miss it. But where are Dave and Kamau?"

"Well, your message said to hurry. We figured we needed help, so Dave and Kamau went back to Rugendo to show our parents and the Cheetahs the way. I came to see if I could catch up with you. Are you sure Matt's down in that hut?"

"I think so," I said, but my confidence was draining away. What if he wasn't there? I changed the subject. "How'd you do on the bridge at the bottom of the ravine?" I asked.

"I stopped and walked my bike over it," Jon answered. "It wasn't too tough. Why?"

I told him about my crash and showed him the purple bruise on my hip. We Rhinos always compared bruises, cuts, and scars.

"That's a great bruise," Jon said, whistling softly. "I'd rate it a 9.8, even better than Matt's when he fell off the rope swing."

Mentioning Matt brought my mind back to the present. "When do you think Dave, Kamau, and the Cheetahs will get here with our parents?" I asked Jon.

"Soon, I hope," he answered. We decided to wait until they came before approaching the hut.

Something moved near the hut. "It looks like Reverend Kimani," I whispered. "I think he's carrying a water jug. Maybe he's going to fetch water." We watched as the figure moved away from the hut.

"Where do you think he's going?" Jon asked.

"I don't know," I answered. "But if he's not in the hut, I think maybe we should go down now and get Matt. Otherwise, even with our dads, someone might get hurt if we have to force our way in."

Jon agreed. "At least we can find out for sure if Matt is really there," he said. We prayed quietly for God to be with us. Jon gave one final piece of advice. "We should run down the path toward the hut crouched over like this." He demonstrated and looked like Quasimodo, the hunchback of Notre Dame. I raised my left eyebrow at the sight. "Just do it," Jon commanded. "Reverend Kimani will have a hard time seeing us even if he turns around and looks back at his little shelter in the cornfield."

Suddenly a stonelike voice erupted from behind the rock. "No for the good!"

CHAPTER THIRTEEN

A MYSTERIOUS STRANGER

We whirled and saw Mwago, his frayed bush hat framing his dark, angry face. He turned from us and his eyes squinted to slits as he stared down the hill. "No for the good," he repeated. "He the no good. He the Mau Mau. He take the *thenge* oath. He steal your friend."

His anger didn't seem to be directed at us, but at Reverend Kimani. I had no idea how Mwago had found his way here from the old cave. "Who is the Mau Mau?" I asked him. "What's the *thenge* oath? And how did you get here?"

The man pointed at his chest proudly and stated, "Me Mwago. Me fight against Mau Mau in forest. You know Aberdare forest? I fight for British. But Queen no give me pension."

"But the fight for independence took place in the 1950s," I told him. "The fight between the British and the Mau Mau is finished."

Mwago scowled at both of us and made a sweeping motion with one hand toward the small shelter in the cornfield. "I kill many Mau Mau. They no like me. Him the Mau Mau." We could see Reverend Kimani's figure disappearing into a nearby ravine. "He take the *thenge* oath, the oath of the male goat. Now he steal your friend. Boy like you. No for the good."

I sucked in a lungful of air and looked at Jon. "If Mwago's right, Matt's in the hut. We should go rescue him now while Reverend Kimani is down in the ravine."

Mwago pointed at the dark forest where the monkeys had clambered high up in a parasol tree. "The forest my home. I fight the Mau Mau." Mwago crouched on his hands and knees like a dog before dropping to his stomach and dragging himself forward by digging his elbows into the ground the way a spider conch digs its foot into the sand to lurch forward. "Me get the Mau Mau," Mwago stated flatly before slithering away.

"He certainly is crazy," said Jon. "We know that Reverend Kimani is not a Mau Mau. But if Mwago thinks Reverend Kimani is a freedom fighter, maybe we can use him to help us rescue Matt."

Jon called out, "Sksss!" The medals on Mwago's hat jangled as he jerked around to look at us. Jon ran over and knelt next to Mwago. "We need your help. That man down there has taken our friend."

Mwago nodded solemnly. "He the Mau Mau. Him take white boy. Him take *thenge* oath."

"Yeah, whatever," Jon agreed. "Listen, we need you to help us rescue our friend. The man's name is Reverend Kimani. . . ."

"No for the good," Mwago interrupted. "He the Mau Mau."

"Yeah, well, anyway," Jon went on, "if you'll follow the man into the ravine and keep him away from the hut, we'll run down and untie our friend and get back up here."

"I kill the Mau Mau," Mwago stated, nodding.

"No, you don't have to kill him," I said, frightened. "We just want you to keep him away from the hut long enough for us to free Matt."

He looked at me for a long time. He stared at my bush hat. Something seemed to click in his mind, and he stood up straight and saluted. "I will do as you command, Sergeant Major." He turned and ran down the hill.

Jon and I looked at each other. "I wonder why he called me Sergeant Major?" I asked.

"Maybe your bush hat makes you look like some soldier from his regiment," Jon answered.

"I hope we did the right thing and he's not dangerous. He said he wanted to kill the Mau Mau. I don't want to think of him killing anyone," I said, shuddering.

"I don't think he will," Jon said. "He doesn't have any weapons. He's just a harmless old crazy man. But we'd better run and find Matt right away while this Mwago guy is distracting Reverend Kimani."

Jon and I raced down the path toward the hut. We saw Mwago disappear into the ravine where Reverend Kimani had gone. We had to hurry. The sun touched the peaks behind us, and we knew we barely had half an hour of daylight left. And we didn't know how long Mwago could keep Reverend Kimani away.

When we reached the hut, we hid behind a bush to catch our breath and listen. No sound came from inside. Hoping it was safe, we crept to the low door and peered in. Matt was there! He wasn't tied up at all, though a sisal rope lay coiled nearby. He sat on a three-legged stool in the corner. This would be an easy rescue.

On seeing us, Matt's mouth opened wide. "Dean! Jon! Boy, am I ever glad to see you two guys!"

We hurried into the hut. I had a million questions to ask, but I knew we had to get Matt out quickly. "Why did Reverend Kimani leave you?" I asked. "Do you know where he went?"

"He went to fetch water. But how'd you find out his name was Reverend Kimani? And how did you trace me here?"

"I'll tell you later," I said. "Right now we have to get you out of here and back home safely."

"But I can't leave without saying good-bye to Reverend Kimani," Matt said. "He'd be worried and wonder what had happened to me."

"What's wrong with your head?" Jon burst out. "The man kidnapped you and has held you hostage for three days. Now we have a chance to make a break for it, and you want to wait and tell him good-bye? Come on, let's go!"

"I tell you, I can't," Matt pleaded with us. "Reverend Kimani is no criminal. Yes, he kidnapped me, but he did it out of fear. I can't just leave. I need to talk with him before we go."

"If you wait to talk with him, he won't let you go, and he won't let us go either. We have to get out now," I argued. "It's almost dark, which is probably why he left you untied. He thought you wouldn't risk going through the forest by yourself at night, but now there are three of us. Come on." I grabbed Matt's hand, and being bigger than he was, I pulled him up and dragged him toward the door.

I became annoyed at his resistance. "Listen, Matt, your kidnapper probably won't be back soon anyway. We sent a crazy Kenyan soldier named Mwago after him. This old guy seems to think Reverend Kimani is a Mau Mau and during Kenya's war for independence Mwago fought the Mau Mau. So he ran after Reverend Kimani. No telling what Mwago will do when he catches up with Reverend Kimani."

Just then we heard a loud yelping scream. Matt turned toward us with fear etched on his face. "Something's happened to Reverend Kimani!" he said. "We have to go help him." He scooted out the door, and Jon and I sprinted to catch up. We could hear shouting down in the thickly forested ravine where both Reverend Kimani and Mwago had gone.

Jon, the fastest runner in the fourth grade class at our missionary school, soon caught up with Matt, but I lagged behind. They slipped into an opening between two large cedar trees, and I followed. The shouting below us grew louder. When I finally caught up, I stopped short. Reverend Kimani lay on the ground as Mwago stood over him, trying to kick him. Matt had jumped on Mwago's back like a baby baboon clinging to its mother. Matt was kicking and punching at Mwago's large back, but the man's tattered old army jacket absorbed the blows. Jon stood to the side, uncertain what to do next.

"Stop it!" I shouted. "Mwago, stop! That's an order!"

At the sound of his name, the crazy old soldier stopped and looked at me. His eyes got a faraway look, and he saluted me. "Yes, Sergeant Major." He stood at attention, seemingly unaware that Matt hung on his back. Matt let go and slipped to the ground before running to Reverend Kimani. I led Mwago aside and ordered him to sit down. Again he saluted and answered, "Yes, Sergeant Major."

"Reverend Kimani, are you OK?" Matt asked as he knelt beside the fallen pastor. Reverend Kimani sat and brushed the dirt and sticks and straw from his clothes. He winced as he touched his side. He stood up, took a deep breath, and said, "I am fine." But he limped slightly as he walked.

Matt apologized for us. "I'm sorry my friends sent that crazy soldier after you. They thought he would delay you so they could help me escape. But I told them I couldn't leave without saying good-bye to you."

Reverend Kimani smiled. He looked at us. "Don't worry. I know Mwago. He fought for the British in the war for independence. I guess this country hasn't been very kind to him since then. He's been living in the forest for years, and he thinks everyone is a Mau Mau. He usually just yells at people instead of attacking them." Reverend Kimani's face looked sad. "But maybe Mwago's right. I deserved to be beaten. Maybe I really am a Mau Mau."

"What do you mean?" I asked.

"Come back to the hut. I will prepare some tea and I will tell you the story."

Matt scrambled to pick up the fallen water jug. He carried it to the brook that burbled along the ravine floor and filled it. Reverend Kimani went over to Mwago and said a few words in Kikuyu. Mwago came and stood beside me.

"*Twende*, let's go, Sergeant Major," Mwago said.

Reverend Kimani whispered to me, "I'm not sure why, but it seems he thinks you're his Sergeant Major from his days in the army. It will be easier for us to pretend it is so. He will follow you and obey all your commands." I nodded.

It seemed strange to have this ragged old soldier marching along behind me and saluting me every time I looked at him, but it was better than having him raging mad. I still didn't understand how Reverend Kimani could have kidnapped Matt and now be acting so nice to Matt and to us. They seemed like friends. No wonder Matt had refused to run away with us.

Back at the hut, we sat down on some low stools that leaned

against the mud walls. The seats were black and shiny from the many backsides that had rested on them over the years. Reverend Kimani poured water into a black-bottomed cooking pot and placed it over the fire, which had a few red coals left. He blew on the fire and added some chunks of firewood.

As he stood back, Matt said, "Before you explain your story, I should introduce you to my friends. This is Dean and this is Jon." We each nodded as our names were mentioned. "They came to rescue me and take me home. But as I said, I refused to leave without talking to you first. They were confused when I wouldn't run away with them."

Mwago, tired from running after Reverend Kimani, fell asleep, and his nostrils quivered as he began to snore in great rumbling gasps. His back slumped against the wall.

Reverend Kimani looked at the old soldier with a smile then began to speak loudly so we could hear him over Mwago's grumbling snorts.

CHAPTER FOURTEEN

REVEREND KIMANI'S STORY

"**W**ell, boys, let me explain why I brought Matt here. I will tell you my story. I am a pastor to about five churches in this area. My home is just on the other side of Makutano. God gave me the ability to preach well. As a result, my name became well known in this area and around the country of Kenya. Many people talked about the beautiful sermons I preached. I've even preached on the radio and the television. I am often invited to speak at seminars and youth camps. In fact, it was at one of those seminars that I first met Matt and his father."

I listened closely. This didn't sound like the voice of a kidnapper. A glance out the door showed me the sun had gone completely. I settled back. We might be here all night. Dave and the others probably couldn't find their way in the dark.

Reverend Kimani continued. "Satan used my speaking ability to trap me. He whispered in my ear that I was a great preacher. I believed him. I became proud. No one could teach me anything. I began to look down on the other pastors in the area and be critical of them. Yes, Satan trapped me with my own pride."

Reverend Kimani paused and bent over in a corner of the house.

I could hear a rattling sound as he rummaged through some old cans. He pulled out a blue kerosene lantern. Matt moved over to help him light the lamp. Matt hung it from a bent nail that was pounded into a shiny soot-blackened wooden rafter pole.

Reverend Kimani leaned forward and poured some milk from a bottle into the boiling water. He sprinkled in some tea leaves, and the mixture slowly turned a golden brown. He signaled to Matt who handed him a brown paper bag. Reverend Kimani shook sugar from this bag into the tea. He picked up a big wooden spoon and gently stirred the Kenyan *chai*.

Sitting back on his stool, he went on. "A few months ago, with the announcement of countrywide elections for our members of parliament, the Kikuyu elders began enforcing oathing. This is when people in my tribe are forced to join with others in sacrificing a goat. They take an oath of loyalty to the tribe. Back in the 1950s the oath was used to unite my people against the colonial government. Many Christians opposed the oath in those troubled days, and some were even killed for refusing to take the oath. The purpose now is political, which isn't so bad, but in the oath we have to swear by the spirits and gods of our past tribal religion. As Christians, we oppose this. Jesus is the only true God. A Christian taking the oath is seen as denying Jesus Christ. I was the loudest in the fight. I spoke out strongly against the oath. One of my messages against the oathing aired on national radio. But you see, I fought the battle in my own strength alone. I had forgotten to turn to the Lord for help."

He paused, a sad look covering his face. His shoulder sagged as he went on. "One night I had a visit from the Kikuyu elders and our local *mundu mugo*. That's someone in our traditional religion who we thought could speak with the Creator God through the spirits. Often you missionaries called these men witch doctors. These men told me I had to take the oath the next day. I wanted to say no, but suddenly fear gripped my heart. I felt cold and alone. I shivered. The *mundu mugo* threatened to put curses on my wife and on my children. He said my wife would have no more children, and he said my children would fail at school. If I had been walking close to the Lord, I would have been able to resist, knowing that Jesus is more powerful than Satan and his evil spirits. But because of my pride, I had stopped turning to the Lord for anything. I tried to do everything by my own power, but my strength failed me at that hour. I agreed to go with the men and take the oath."

"So it *was* you we saw that day near Rugendo when we saw the oathing ceremony," I said.

"Yes," he answered sadly. "And when I saw Matt, I was sure he'd recognized me. I thought he would tell his father, and I would be thrown out of the church. I was so afraid. I just wanted to make sure no one found out how I had failed the Lord.

"Then I visited my cousin, the pastor at Rugendo, to make arrangements for when I was scheduled to preach there the next Sunday. As I left Rugendo, I saw you boys on your bicycles, and on an impulse I decided to follow you. I went into the forest. When I saw you returning, I hid."

I turned to Matt. "I told you I saw someone that day when we first rode up the old slave trail." Matt nodded. We both looked back at Reverend Kimani.

He continued, "I didn't think any of you had seen me that time, but when I preached the next Sunday I felt so afraid. I saw Matt sitting there, and I was certain he would tell his dad he'd seen me at the oathing ceremony. I decided as I preached I would have to do something to stop Matt from talking."

Matt shook his head. "I had to confess to Reverend Kimani this afternoon that I wasn't paying too much attention to his sermon that day. I was busy counting wood-boring beetle holes in the church rafters. To tell the truth, I'd almost forgotten about the oathing ceremony."

Reverend Kimani went on. "That afternoon, I heard my cousin's son, Ben, talking about a bike race. I knew you boys were involved. I looked at the map of the race that Ben had. I remembered a place I'd seen in the woods the day I followed you, and I thought it would be a perfect chance to kidnap Matt. I didn't want to hurt him, but I had to make sure he didn't speak to his dad about the oathing ceremony. After jumping out and pulling Matt into the ravine, I left his bike and a phony ransom note where I hoped someone might find it. If people thought I was hiding near enough to collect ransom money, they'd never look for me so far away. I hurried here where I hid Matt in this hut. When I ran out of food, I left Matt tied up this morning and borrowed a bike to go buy some food for him at the Rugendo *duka*. I didn't dare buy things in Makutano. People might have been suspicious. But today has been so hard. I've had to tell so many lies to cover up my sin. I have felt so guilty. When I got back I told Matt the whole story."

"Once I heard how sorry Reverend Kimani was for what he'd done, I wasn't sure what to say," said Matt. "But I knew I had to forgive him. So I did."

"I was amazed when he forgave me completely," Reverend Kimani said.

I looked at Matt, his eyes staring at the floor. I guess he was embarrassed.

Matt looked up. "I told Reverend Kimani we all make mistakes, but God forgives us if we admit we've sinned and pray for forgiveness. Remember? We learned 1 John 1:9 a few weeks ago in Sunday school. I reminded Reverend Kimani about how Peter denied Jesus, too. Not once, but three times. But Jesus forgave him and used him. Just this afternoon Reverend Kimani prayed and confessed his sin, first for taking the oath and then for kidnapping me to cover up his sin."

Reverend Kimani shook his head sadly. "First Corinthians 4:5 talks about how God will bring to light what we have tried to hide from Him and will expose the motives of our hearts. God has convicted me of my pride and lack of trust."

Matt grinned. "When he stood up after confessing all that, I knew he was a changed man. He went to get some water for our tea, and you guys showed up to rescue me with your crazy soldier there. Now you know why I couldn't leave."

Jon and I nodded. It was quite a story. The tea began to boil, and Reverend Kimani gripped the outer edges of the top of the pot and removed it from the fire. He swished it one more time with a yellow plastic tea strainer, then poured the *chai* through the strainer into white enamel mugs with painted red and yellow flowers on the sides. I nudged Mwago and gave him a mug. He grunted his thanks and drank his *chai* in loud thirsty slurps. The *chai* tasted warm and sweet.

"So how did you guys find me?" Matt asked. We told him our story. Reverend Kimani laughed quietly when we told him about following the unique track made by the tire of the bicycle he had borrowed.

Just then we heard barking and voices outside. Mwago, eyes bulging, leaped to his feet, spilling his *chai*. "The Mau Mau come!" he hissed urgently. He ran from the hut before any of us could grab him.

When we looked out, we could see no sign of Mwago. "I hope he'll be OK," I said.

"Don't worry," Reverend Kimani replied. "He'll probably run back to his hideout in the forest. I think he's had enough excitement for one day."

We looked up the hill and saw an army of lights. The barking and baying grew closer. "Dave must have brought everyone from Rugendo," Jon commented.

Reverend Kimani's eyes opened wide with fear. "I don't like dogs," he said.

Matt held his arm gently. "Don't worry, Reverend Kimani. We'll make sure nothing happens to you." But how could we be sure? As a kidnapper he could go to jail or even be whipped ten strokes with a hippo-hide whip! They did that kind of thing in the Kenyan courts.

We stepped away from the hut and called out, "We're over here!"

Within minutes the missionaries and Kenyans from Rugendo reached the hut. Matt's mom and dad led the way. Seeing Matt, they rushed in and hugged him. Usually we Rhinos aren't much for tears or hugs, but this night they seemed to come without warning. When I saw Matt's mom crying and hugging Matt, I started to cry with happiness. She kept repeating, "Matt! You're safe! You're safe!"

Suddenly my father's strong arms enveloped me. I hugged him back. "I see you found your friend," he said. I nodded through my